BEACH CAT

AND

THE WISDOM OF THE ORANGE

James West

authorHOUSE®

AuthorHouse™
1663 Liberty Drive, Suite 200
Bloomington, IN 47403
www.authorhouse.com
Phone: 1-800-839-8640

First published by AuthorHouse 10/16/2008

ISBN: 978-1-4343-6864-5 (e)
ISBN: 978-1-4343-6863-8 (sc)

Printed in the United States of America
Bloomington, Indiana

This book is printed on acid-free paper.

About the Author

Quite some time ago, James West had a yearning to become a cartoonist. Eventually, his thoughts would evolve into a mystical short story for both young readers and adults alike.

Ironically, because he has Attention Deficit Disorder and is not an avid reader himself, the middle-aged Mr. West found the art of writing to be quite difficult. Nonetheless, by employing the old adage of 'practice makes perfect,' the author developed a technique that not only keeps the reader's interest and makes them crave for more, but also allows for greater retention of subject matter. Consequently, sentence structuring and scenic literature takes on new meaning. Anything but boring, his work is exciting - it 'JUMPS' right out at you!

Acknowledgments

First and foremost…to the trinity of the great and almighty Wisdom, his watchful spirit, and his unforgettable son himself, whose saving graces will always be there for the taking.

Honorable mention…to my Florida connections and influences of Frank, Brad, Sue, Nancy, Marcy, Sandy #1, sunbathing Sandy #2 and her friendly beach cat visitor…and to Debby, Marsha, Diana, Renee, Sarah, Sandra, Melissa, Dilan, Melanie, Chuck, Phil and Joe in Lockport, N.Y.

Introduction

Someday, if you're fortunate, you may run across Beach Cat, an extremely friendly and distinctive feline of the Maine Coon variety. In case you were wondering, he lives near an ocean, where he takes his allotted place in society. Bearing supernatural abilities, this 'chosen' animal is a pillar of his community, contributing whatever help and protection he can to the needy. Which is to say, when challenged by either calamity or adversity, ordinarily, his eyes change color and his body begins to grow. As a result, astounding strength and gumption he most certainly will show. If called for, from his long curvaceous claws, incredible defensive and constructive powers are able to flow!

Beach Cat acquired his special traits after being sprayed by the juice of an orange, which split-open beside him after falling from a tree. The colorful dimpled orb was struck by a heavenly bolt of lightning as God meant for it to be. Thus, when the Maine Coon licked his fur and ingested some of the fruit's spiritually altered nectar, all at once, 'BAZOOM,' his fifteen-pound physical structure began to change! In a flash, his green-colored eyes turned orange and he started to feel all tingly and strange. Upon doubling in size and having been endowed with the might of a tiger, his spark-emitting front claws tripled in length, filling with consummate weapons of supercharged lightning and pliable forces that were humanely designed for healing. To say the least, his unexpected divine experience was quite invigorating!

Immediately following his transformation, ostensibly, from the grounded orange, he heard a commanding voice, which delivered an awesome revelation. It was a message from God, who addressed a bedazzled Beach Cat in a way no one else could hear. "Now that you've been sanctified as one of my worldly guardian angels," said the Lord, "your responsibilities are to care for the meek and disadvantaged… and to rightfully and bravely uphold justice, for evil aggression and earthly devices you are not to fear. However, as with all my other angels in their respective areas, you will have strict rules to revere! Put your undivided trust in me and listen carefully," directed the Almighty. "Initially, come what may, to earn my good favor, you must practice patience, abide by and distribute my teachings, and make every effort to give life your best. Such virtues are endearing to me and will be your most primary everyday tests! Secondly, when you find yourself in a precarious way or somehow mired in dismay, in order to draw on your built-in uplifting strength and both your claw-based healing energy and armament of lightning, you must first seek my knowledge…which means you'll have to pray."

For future assistance, the Creator schooled Beach Cat on what to ask for and what to say. "Eternal Wisdom," he began, "in my weak, dark, and yearning hour, give me courage and stability. If necessary, bestow upon me your supremacy…amen!"

"At my discretion," continued God, "through that prayer, my ever-present spirit, and the enriched 'Vitamin C' that bonds you with me, you may realize some, all, or none of your angelic skill. Whatever my offering or communiqué happens to be, assuredly, it'll fortify your spiritual will. Just keep this in mind, oh mighty cat…always heed my wisdom, for it's good advice…truly, it will suffice. Most importantly, once you've managed to master all I ask of you, that'll be the day when you join me in never ending paradise! Henceforth, until you summon me from your planetary setting, I'll be busy elsewhere, but my spirit will persist. Indeed, it'll remain to judge your progress, rate my response to your worthiness and wants, and keep me informed of everything you do…so, go now and take my blessings and wisdom with you."

After God stopped talking, Beach Cat's body returned to normal and he was off and running! Feeling somewhat dazed, the naive animal was totally amazed that a piece of fruit had spoken to him. Consequently, on an innocent whim, he thought of God as the 'Wisdom of the Orange.'

As the excited feline headed for his neighborhood domicile and its relaxing waterfront view, he was anxious to inform his friends about his unbelievable experience…a story that would ring true!

Beach Cat's pals include Peter the pelican, a Golden Retriever called Dune Dog, and a silly turtle and crab named Fred and Charlie. Collectively, they all reside in a cave. Their outdoor-indoor house was something nature had made. From there, the blithe animals like to roam. Along with another close acquaintance, lifeguard Larry, they all chose Sunset Beach as their home.

Now, it's time to join the group and their escapades into the unknown!

'SPLASH ~ BAM ~ WHAM!' crashed the wave-skimming jet ski.

~ ~ ~ ~ ~ ~ ~ ~ ~

"Faster...we wanna go faster!" shouted the speedboat's passengers.

~ ~ ~ ~ ~ ~ ~ ~ ~

"Mommy, can I have a cold soda?" asked little five-year-old Emma.
"Help yourself, baby," encouraged her sunbathing mother. "Just keep your drink on top of the cooler so you'll know where its at!"
"Okay, I will," replied Emma. "Thank you, mommy...I love you lots and lots and lots!"
"I love you too, baby!" acknowledged the youngster's smiling guardian.

It was in the heart of July, and although it was getting late in the day, Sunset Beach and its warm ocean waters continued to bustle with activity. On that particular Saturday, a large horde of people had gathered for all sorts of recreation at their beloved Florida resort.

Sitting amid the die-hard shoreline crowd was a wide-eyed and vibrant Beach Cat, who was flanked by his friends, Dune Dog and Peter the pelican. The three animals lived in an age-old cave near the water and for the most part, relished what their tropical locale had to offer. Like so many times in the past, it was presently their sole topic of conversation. "Boy, I sure wish I had that sleek-looking speedboat out there!" announced Beach Cat. "I've seen it around here before. It'd be a rave to ride in it...its got moo-cho get up and go!"

"Yeah, well I'd prefer to have the jet ski," proclaimed Dune Dog. "I've been watching it bounce through the wake of that speedboat! Talk about bucking broncos, taking a spin on one of them would probably make me sea sick...but I'd still wanna give it a try!"

Being less meticulous, an impartial Peter wasn't picking any favorites. "I wouldn't mind having both of those high-performance machines," revealed the pelican. "I'd be in my glory with them. Hey, now you guys know what you can get me for my birthday!"

Out of curiosity, 'SWOOSH ~ SWOOSH ~ SWOOSH,' Peter flapped his long wings and took to the air in order to pursue and get a bird's-eye-view of the busy aquatic vessels.

While the mesmerized trio dwelled on the commotion in the ocean, their other live-in companions, Charlie the Stone Crab and Fred the Loggerhead Turtle were currently milling-about at home. Having caught too many rays from the sun, the two scorched sea critters, who'd just left the beach scene, were looking to refresh themselves in a mini salt water and spring-fed pond that was located at the center of their cave. With an eager Fred already taking the plunge, Charlie hurriedly crawled to the rear of their rocky abode, where he raised one of his front claws to click-on Dune Dog's dusty battery-powered boom box. He then cranked-up his spindly legs, and to the rhythm of some good-time music, he made a mad dash for the inviting seventy-degree swimming hole.

Egging him on was his talkative and happily-sighing turtle friend. "Ahhh…this cold water really puts out the fire on my hot shell!" bellowed Fred. "Man, you need to get in here, Charlie…it's total ecstasy…it'll make ya feel fantastic! I uh…I expect you're tired of me mentioning that if we were clever, we'd start selling tickets for this indoor pool of ours. Yeah, I'd wager all the scummy algae on my belly that some of those half baked beach-goers we stepped on a minute ago would buy 'em!"

During his approach, Charlie played off of his cohort's comments, starting with the hundred-pound Loggerhead's overheated body. "Wow…you're the one who's half baked, Fred!" expressed the crab. "Your shell is steaming like a tea kettle! You're so hot, I could press a shirt with you…which makes me think…if we were clever, we'd open a laundry business and you could do all the ironing. You'd just love to put creases in clothes by the basketful, wouldn't ya? Anyhow, dude, I'm not interested in selling tickets for our pond or running any kind of an enterprise…I just wanna extinguish the same fire on me that was burnin' on you. So gang-way…I only have a few feet to go before I reach what you call total ecstasy!"

In Charlie's haste to get into his home away from the ocean, he missed the turtle spooning his open mouth below the pond's surface. Using his now tightly closed beak for a squirt gun, Fred raised his head, breathed deeply through his nose, and 'SPLAT,' he pummeled the crab's face with a hard stream of water. "Ouch - Oooch - Ouch!" cried a recoiling Charlie. "Fred, ya schmuck! Whatta ya…whatta ya think you're doing?"

"Oh, I was just rinsing a clump of sand from your dirty puss," replied the turtle. "What a rush, huh?"

Stunned by the rude and wet surprise, Charlie didn't realize he was being toyed with and angrily voiced his displeasure. "Fred, whatta ya talking about? My face was nice and clean!"

The impish Loggerhead was quick to polish-off his soggy little gag. "In that case, Charlie, you'd better check whatever fell to the ground. It pains me to tell ya this, but I think I just dislodged one of your eyeballs. As a matter of fact, I can see it staring up at you…its giving you the once-over…it probably can't believe it came from something as nerdy-looking as you!"

Now aware of his sidekick's charade, the Stone Crab 'clacked' his powerful front claws in a menacing manner and cut-loose with a cantankerous comeback. "Fred, once I'm in the pond, I'm gonna lop-off your stinky scaly feet and shove them into your mouth! It should keep ya from shooting water at me. Besides that, with your feet stuffed under your nose, you'll have to smell them all the time!"

"Charlie, if anyone's gonna smell my feet, it'll be you," retorted the turtle. "Yeah, as soon as you get in here, I'm gonna stick them straight in your repulsive face!"

"Go for it, Fred!" urged the oncoming crab. "While you're tryin' to play footsy with my mug, I'll be paring the green skin off your dumb ol' cucumber head. Now, quit yapping and stand back…I'm coming in for a big belly-floppin' dip!"

When they were finished with their spirited swim, Charlie and Fred were planning on taking their second nap of the day. Afterward, they were going to wait for their dog, cat, and pelican friends to join them in their wide-bellied cave, which was semi-hidden below a long line of elevated beach cottages, high-rise condominiums, and luxurious to no-frills lodgings for tourists and travelers.

As far as their communal household goes, before their four-year tenure with one another, the stray companions living arrangements all came about through somewhat tragic circumstances. Relatively speaking, first among them to inhabit Sunset Beach was Dune Dog, who in his distraught juvenile and mid-life days went by the name of Burps. While having anything but fun and being fresh on the run from his abusive owner in the suburban part of town, he took a soothing walk along the ocean and happened to meet-up with a blond-haired lifeguard named Larry Lawson, who not only resided, but also worked in the vicinity. Upon conversing with soiled six-year-old Burps and hearing of his problems, which entailed frequent beatings, exposure, and shockingly, alcohol consumption, all prior to taking him under his roof that night, Larry gave the intoxicated and limping Golden Retriever something to eat, tweezed a prickly sandspur from his front paw, and by means of his garden hose and a thorough soapy scrubbing, he literally showered him with an overdue grooming from head to tail!

Regardless of his immediate desire to make shaggy and likable Burps a permanent fixture around his shoreline bungalow, before sunrise, Larry's forgotten but fast-emerging allergies to animal fur preempted such an arrangement. Consequently, to furnish the dog with an alternative haven, both the wheezing and sneezing lifeguard pulled some strings with local government and moved him into a nearby common-area cave on the beach. From then on, along with installing a protective wooden door on the cave's smallish entrance, Larry supplied Burps with an abundant flow of food and water. Throwing in a couple of housewarming presents, he gave him a new fleece blanket to sleep on and brought over an old portable radio for entertainment purposes. Making sure the canine stayed on the wagon, one thing Larry didn't provide for him was a bowl full of bubbly beer, which is what his former so-called caregiver had served him on a daily basis. Indeed, doing his best to revamp things, the lifeguard then took to scrapping Burps' alcohol-related name. Fittingly, because the cave allotted to him was encased by a tall sand dune, Larry labeled him, Dune Dog. The catchy title was prized by the Golden Retriever, who was mutually enamored with his new digs. Five'll get ya ten, his life was on the upswing!

In maximizing his high and broadening his horizons, Dune did a lot of exploring and became a mainstay on the open beach, where he kept company with Larry and learned all there was to know about his job. Remarkably, after agreeing to and undergoing a rigorous amount of training, which included extensive use of his teeth, the intelligent dog was soon swimming and working beside his lifeguard instructor, helping him with rescues and other significant tasks. The educational experience was truly rewarding for Dune, whose developing skills were much appreciated by Larry.

As he began to come into his own, Dune assimilated and familiarized himself with many of the regular beach-goers as well. When not around Larry, he was mingling and visiting with others, making friends left and right! During his socializing, he was also keeping an eye out for any signs of disorderly conduct or potential safety hazards. To wit, they were other basic branches of his training.

Deflating to him always having plenty to do and someone to hang with during daylight hours, at sundown, when the beach was quiet and an off-duty Larry was away courting his girlfriend, Dune wallowed in boredom and loneliness. Forlornly, talking to the odd passerby or listening to the music on his stereo just wasn't doing the trick and he was starting to get the blues!

One particular dull evening, after falling asleep, he had a disturbing dream concerning some inclement weather that was threatening Sunset Beach. His nightmare appeared to be an omen of things to come and would fuel his budding depression, for within that bleak month of September, a tropical storm sideswiped and hammered the region! Forced to evacuate his cave, all morning long, Dune sat with Larry in his besieged and blacked-out cottage, where they waited for the radical combination of howling wind, heavy rains, and rising ocean waters to subside.

Later in the day, after the storm crept inland and took a powder in central Florida, amongst an assorted mass of washed-up seaweed, driftwood, and lifeless globular jellyfish, three debilitated but alive creatures turned up on the eroded sands of Sunset Beach. One of them happened to be an adult pelican named Peter, who was totally disoriented and could do nothing but flop around on the wet ground. Unfortunately, while engaged in a last-minute fishing trip, the famished bird was thrashed by the storm's gusty winds and blown against the trunk of a shoreline palm tree. Suffering from a slight concussion, Peter had absolutely no idea of where he was or what he was doing.

Simultaneously, lying near the pelican was a large fifty-pound turtle named Fred. At the time, Fred had his lightweight buddy, Charlie the crab precariously perched atop his broad-shelled back. Earlier, as a result of being chased by a shark and venturing into shallow water, the twosome had been tossed and beaten-about by the heaving ocean. Its incoming tide eventually ferried them onto the beach. That was only the half of it, for somewhere along their topsy-turvy ride, they'd gotten entangled with a mesh of old fishing line and were literally tied to one another. To make matters even worse, a portion of the thin nylon cord was tightly coiled around Fred's neck. Seeing stars and losing color in his face told that he was having trouble breathing, especially with an on-board Charlie struggling to free himself. Their abysmal situation was clearly inescapable. In order to survive, they would be needing outside intervention!

Meanwhile, as Charlie, Fred, and Peter lay under the torrid Florida sun, their plight was noticed by Dune Dog, who in combo with Larry was autonomously roaming and inspecting the shoreline. Once he'd made contact and had given Fred and Charlie an innate precautionary sniffing, Dune put his teeth to work and carefully stripped the fishing line away from their bonded bodies. Following his liberating and exchanging brief introductions with the grateful worse-for-wear duo, Dune politely invited them over to his cave for a little rest and relaxation. His kind gesture went over well and was wholly accepted! At that juncture, the Golden Retriever terminated his beach maneuvers and traipsed over to Peter, where he used his snout to prod and steer the injured pelican toward his cave. During his time consuming trip, he had the slow-crawling turtle and crab in tow.

Upon their arrival at Dune's previously flooded waterfront home, conveniently, Fred and Charlie made themselves comfortable in the cave's two-foot-deep kidney shaped pond. Likewise, after staggering around the sodden rock-strewn grounds, Peter selected an attractive-looking spot close to the cave's door and plopped down on Dune's soft dampened blanket.

Whilst recovering and taking pleasure in their private surroundings, the turtle, crab, and pelican not only spent hours talking and warming up to one another, but also took the opportunity to get chummy with their accommodating canine host. In correlation, Dune was accumulating a feel for and worming information from his sea-faring guests. In addition to him hearing about their brush with the storm and listening to other personal stories, he learned that Fred and Charlie had recently moved from the remote Bahama Islands and were searching for a new place to occupy. On a more local level, Peter happened to be indigenous to the coastal town of Reddington Shores, a mere hop, skip, and jump from Sunset Beach.

Concerning the multiple personalities he was dealing with, Dune found himself pulled from the doldrums and kept in stitches by Fred and Charlie. To the dog's delight, they both loved to tell jokes and were able to come up with a funny adlib to go along with just about anything being discussed. Aside from that, due to his inexperience with the turtle and crab's past, Dune was unaware that their seemingly positive sense of humor had always been plagued by negative repercussions. It was something which would definitely be a cause for concern in the future!

In analyzing Peter, who wasn't adept at telling jokes, but could be dryly funny ala his droll lingo, Dune really liked his gregarious demeanor. Excluding the bump on his head, other impressive features about the pelican were his honest and down-to-earth thoughts; that is, when his brain-rattling concussion began to wane and his foggy thinking processes were less inhibited!

Overall, from their impromptu meeting, everyone hit-it-off extremely well. Going with his intuition, Dune was compelled to offer his novel friends permanent refuge in his one-room cathedral ceiling domain. Fortunately, they all consented to his proposal and the retriever was ecstatic over the fact he'd no longer have to go it alone. Subsequently, the cave now had four occupants.

Right off the bat, via Dune Dog, Peter, Fred and Charlie would get to know and befriend Larry. As well as giving the lifeguard extra company during his work days, to a certain degree, between acclimating themselves to the area, they'd do whatever they could to assist him with his job. In the long haul, because of this unorthodox and diversified man, animal, and sea critter coalition, Sunset Beach was destined to become one of the most unique and popular resorts in all of Florida! Before earning its accolades, however, one more piece to the puzzle was required.

A year or so later, last to come along and make that monumental impact was a wild scar-faced Maine Coon Cat, whose name was Slasher. Having been abducted from a marina, Slasher was roughed-up, sealed in a plastic bag, and thrown into the waters off of Sunset Beach by an unscrupulous pair of cat-hating boaters. The poor creature was drowning when Dune Dog spotted him in the ocean, swam to his aid, and dragged him into shore. From there, lifeguard Larry acted on Dune's find by transporting the fading feline over to a nearby animal shelter, where his girlfriend, Jennifer James worked as a veterinarian.

Luckily, through Jennifer's intense doctoring, tender loving care, and a resilient one-in-a-million turnaround, in only a matter of a few weeks, the two-year-old cinnamon and gray-colored tomcat was able to make a full recovery. Then again, when his allotted time at the shelter began to run on empty and euthanasia was looming right around the corner for him, Slasher needed to find another place to hang his hat, and fast!

As fate would dictate, once they became aware of the cat's impasse, Dune and his companions gave him yet one more chance at life by voting to adopt him into their group. Upon presenting their decision to Larry, he made an eleventh-hour call to his animal doctor gal-pal, who quickly scratched Slasher's lethal injection. That same day, on her way home from work, Jennifer drove over to the beach and delivered her furry package in person.

Consistent with all probabilities and profound differences, the ensuing atmosphere in the shared cave was initially a bit tense! Nonetheless, an obviously nervous and independent standoffish Slasher, who'd been accustomed to living by himself in the woods was still treated to some pleasant camaraderie and great hospitality. Thankfully enjoying the same handling as Dune Dog, along with a new blanket to bed-down on, he was set up with ample food and water by lifeguard Larry.

Sequentially, when the dust began to settle and Larry and the others managed to get moderately acquainted with the tough-acting animal, they became indebted to him for his willingness to help them patrol the beach and participate in life-saving drills and authentic rescues. Without question, their demanding and often sweltering past-time turned out to be an excellent ice-breaker. In essence, it forged many an interesting conversation between the five cave-dwellers late into the night, with an enthused Slasher doing most of the talking! Slowly but surely, he was adjusting to and making the most of his once-foreign surroundings.

Ultimately, the friendly growing tufted-eared tomcat, who'd led a hard confrontational existence, would adjust to and make the most of what Dune Dog had voluntarily accepted from Larry. That being, a significant modification to his begotten identity. With Dune and the rest of Slasher's close-quarter mates justifiably disturbed by his name, which the sharp-clawed critter acquired from past skirmishes with rival felines, they all opted for something more civilized and void of any nerve wracking hints of hostility. Following them holding a comprehensive conference and exchange of ideas, they affably dubbed the latest and final addition to their family, Beach Cat! Ironically, among other things, it would be a Godsend to Slasher, who incidentally was never fond of his callous call-sign in the first place.

Not long thereafter, on a clear moonlit night, while a newly-christened and out on the town Beach Cat was walking under a neighborhood citrus tree, all at once, an enormous loose-hanging orange fell from its overhead perch and crashed beside him! Instantly, 'SPLAT,' his hairy torso was coated by its sticky and strange-looking fluorescent juice.

Just minutes in advance, through God's direction and underlying future intentions, the orange was pierced and had its chemical composition augmented by an influential fingerling of space-born lightning. The next segment of the Lord's plan was now about to unfold, for as an irritated Beach Cat tongued his fur and wet his whistle with the fruit's acidic ionized nectar, suddenly, 'BR-R-RUMBLE,' loud reverberating thunder pervaded the cloudless sky!

9

In the aftermath of the startling noise, the Maine Coon began to experience all kinds of physical changes. Before he knew what was happening, his hazel eyes turned bright orange, his electrified body grew to a sizeable thirty-pounds, and to the partial subsidy of his metamorphosis, he assumed the strength of a full-grown tiger. Accentuating that, his new elongated front claws were not only outfitted with special healing powers, but were also bristling with defensive weapons of plasmatic energy! When his magnanimous makeover was complete, through a mind-linked connection, he was given an explanation and straight forward instructions by a mysterious voice which seemed to be emanating from the grounded and glowing orange.

Unbeknownst to an overwhelmed Beach Cat, the vital event placed him in the graceful hands of God, who similar to lifeguard Larry was bullish about recruiting someone to help him take care of business; specifically, spiritual business!

Hence, once the animal was appointed as the guardian angel of Sunset Beach and briefed on what was expected of him, expediently, 'FOOM,' his souped-up physique returned to its natural state. However, from then on, whenever he found himself in a quandary or somehow unable to fulfill his pious duties, beneficially, he had an open door policy that allowed him to fall-back-on and find peace of mind in the Creator's sustaining all-knowing wisdom. On those given occasions, more often than not, it resurrected his hidden heavenly powers and afforded him the authority to right any wrongs and thwart sinister upheaval. It also gave him the ability to mend bodily wounds and rid the sick of their worldly afflictions. Never meant to be abused or used frivolously, his persuasive powers were available to him only when they were earned and / or if God deemed them necessary!

Not surprisingly, the terse talk and endorsement he'd received from the Almighty for the purpose of dispensing his good will was something the unpretentious feline had difficulty comprehending. No matter, it would all be immaterial, for as long as he lived a decent optimal life and said a particular prayer, his desires were always met by what he called the 'Wisdom of the Orange.'

Admirably, because of Beach Cat's divine gifts and the strong but flexible character he exhibited, he soon became a household topic and an influential kingpin around Sunset Beach. By and large, this launched the beginning of an innovative and intriguing life for the Maine Coon and those who'd grown close to him; and considered him to be their leader!

With adventure now forthcoming, far from the cave where pond-swimming Fred the turtle and Charlie the crab were pampering themselves, an outdoors Beach Cat and Dune Dog had just laid down on the shady side of a small tiki hut. Located near the shoreline, the raised stilted shelter was lifeguard Larry's headquarters. It was where he spent the majority of his occupational hours and to no wonder, he was presently in-house.

Quite proud to be the owner of an Olympic gold medal, Larry once reigned as the world's fastest freestyle swimmer! Upon bringing home his prestigious award, dubiously, he chose to forego the high profile habits and rich income of a celebrity in favor of returning to his questionably less stressful lifeguard job on the beach. Besides being underpaid and pitiful poor, his pension for basking in the sun and tooling around in the water at his leisure was second nature to him. Not to mention, he thoroughly enjoyed living in his comfy patriotically-painted red, white, and blue beach cottage, which was back-bordered by an ensemble of majestic palm trees and an ocean-linking expanse of *sparkling* white sand.

Through the years, Larry also enjoyed his association with the cave-dwellers, especially Beach Cat. Though he figured the feline's extraordinary powers actually came from God and not a talking piece of fruit, he never disputed the Wisdom of the Orange theory. On a mixed note, the entire concept amused him; yet, because he was privy to many of the animal's miraculous acts, which included the healing of a beach-goers disfigured limb and the annihilation of both a trespassing alligator and an insidious shore-prowling shark, Larry always took the so-called Wisdom's presence seriously!

Still full of energy at thirty-years-old, the lean and tall six-foot-two lifeguard was in his normal upbeat mood. Equipped with his strapped-on, well-used, and decrepit childhood folk guitar, he was hankering to share a few chords of his musical hobby with his distinctly lounging Maine Coon and Golden Retriever friends. Sporting his freshly trimmed mop-top haircut and trademark sky-blue eyes, Larry peered through the open rear window of his tiki hut and collared their attention. "Hey, you guys…I wrote a new song last night…its short but sweet! I already ran it by a bunch of girls earlier and they really went for it. You just might go for it too! Would ya be interested in hearing it or not?"

"Sure!" responded Beach Cat. "I'd love to hear it!"

"R-R-RUFFA...Go ahead!" barked Dune. "Let 'er rip!" he urged.

Operating off the canine's cue, "UH-UMMM," Larry cleared his throat, swept his plastic pick across the strings of his acoustical instrument, and sang his tropical melody.

'STRUMMA ~ STRUM ~ STRUMMITY ~ STRUM ~ STRUM'
"I've got sand under my toes and salt on my tongue
I'm living on the beach and having fun
STRUMMA ~ STRUM ~ STRUM
Love the water / love the sun
Wouldn't give it up for anything or anyone
STRUMMA ~ STRUM ~ STRUM
I'm a happy-go-lucky man / who likes to get a tan
Life's as easy as chewing gum
Yeah man / there's nothing better than being a beach bum"
'STRUMMA ~ STRUM ~ STRUMMITY ~ STRUM ~ STRUM'

At the conclusion of Larry's opus, his impressed companions craved for an encore. "Sing it again," encouraged Beach Cat; "you've got me hooked on it!"

"Ditto!" said Dune. "That's a nifty tune…I think I'm ready for Karaoke!"

Both laughing and jesting, Larry was more than willing to repeat his performance. "HA ~ HA! I'll let ya have another swig from the trough," he offered. "When I'm through, you guys can get in line and for posterity, I'll uh…I'll sign a couple of worthless autographs for ya!"

As Larry interlocked his fingers, cracked his knuckles, and proceeded to give his shoreline mini-concert one last go-around, simultaneously, out over the ocean, Peter the pelican had just signed-off from his chase involving the speedboat and jet ski. Giving his chronic hunger precedence, he was now committed to and flirting with catching himself a fresh fish dinner. Nothing could tempt his taste for fine delicacies more than the squiggling school of Speckled Sea Trout in the water below. "Eureka...there they blow!" he muttered. "I can take whatever one I want!"

In anticipation of a satisfying and cinch meal, 'KA-LOP,' Peter snapped his hard tapered choppers, lowered his wing flaps, and soared downward. Exhibiting superb form, 'SPLOOP,' he executed a perfect minimal ripple high-dive into the ocean.

Dismayingly, after gliding under water and surfacing, his long bill was empty, meaning his intended prey had escaped. "Crummy coconuts!" grumbled the pelican. "Either I'm getting to be too slow and losing my touch or those fish are becoming faster and more cunning. Next time, I'd better bring along a casting net!"

Although Peter had his mind attuned to filling his empty stomach, real soon, his appetite and young-in-the-tooth angling excursion would be suppressed by an unstable phenomenon that was malevolently brewing in the outlying sky! Until the such said incident would befall him, however, he pumped his wings, ascended from the water, and continued his coastal hunt for fish.

Meanwhile, staying busy inside his lifeguard station, a shirtless and bathing suit clad Larry had put up his guitar and was currently tweaking his binoculars through the hut's front window. As he brought them into focus and scanned the water and adjoining beach, everything within his jurisdiction appeared to be satisfactory. The results of his long-range observations compelled him to retrace his barefooted steps and voice his contentment to a backyard Beach Cat and Dune dog. "Thus far, boys, our status is looking good...much better than yesterday, when we had more than our share of problems! Ya know, it's great not having any injuries, rescues, or beach-goer spats to deal with for a change. To garnish it off, weather-wise, its been superb! I've heard diverse predictions of what we were supposed to get today, and the hard evidence amounts to this...we've had no precipitation, the humidity's been quite bearable, and according to the hut's thermometer, the high was only eighty-five! Considering we're in the middle of summer, that's a little on the chilly side…but for me, it's just right…I could go for this kind of heat year round!"

"I'll have to agree with everything you said, Larry," chimed-in Beach Cat; "except for the weather! It's still way too hot for me and I can't wait for wintertime. However, for now, it's nice to get a break from those mid-ninety temperatures! Even more desirable, we're starting to get a lot of overcast, which is fine with me. Hopefully, some of those clouds will block-out the sun and shave a few degrees off the thermometer. All in all though, its been an exceptional day for us and I shouldn't have any complaints."

Dune Dog had something to say about their absent turtle and crab friends. "Our day was good," confirmed the retriever, "but I know for a fact that Fred and Charlie were outside too long and got themselves a bad sunburn! Get this…if you can fathom their stupidity…for the better part of the afternoon, those two barnacle-heads were scavenging for clams in the sand and doing their garbage picking and babe-watching with Peter. They then made the ultimate mistake of falling asleep on the beach. I didn't wanna disturb their beauty rest, so I never bothered to wake 'em up! HARF ~ HARF ~ HARF…anyway," said the chuckling canine, "I could tell they were hurting by the way I saw 'em scrambling for their pond. Talk about stampedes, I'll bet they ran over a few sunbathers on their way back to the cave!"

A smiling bushy-tailed Beach Cat embellished on Dune's observation. "Man…you're not exaggerating about Fred and Charlie's sunburn! Their shells had all the look of kettled potato chips. Personally, I'd much rather deal with hairballs!"

During the group's ensuing laughter to the Maine Coon's explicitness, Larry happened to read the clock in his hut and realized it was almost quitting time. In keeping with his end of the work-day routine, before retiring to his choice local restaurant for a night-cap and then phoning his girl, Jennifer from home, he planned on taking a brisk jog and cool-down walk along the shoreline. Stopping to visit with any willing or talkative beach-goers was also part of his ritual. Prior to his impending departure, the dedicated lifeguard, who was putting in an extensive ten-hour seasonal shift, hoped to get a favor from his two four-legged companions. "Attention dudes!"

14

he beckoned. "If you can pardon me for cutting-short our chit-chat, I'm gonna be closing-up shop within the next thirty minutes, which means I'm about to hit the old cardio silica treadmill. While I'm doing my fast shuffle off to Buffalo, would you guys mind babysitting my aft end?"

"No, not at all, Larry," replied Beach Cat. "Feel free to perspire and give your heart a stress test!"

"Yeah, say no more," uttered Dune; "we'd be honored to cover your caboose…and when ya get to Buffalo, don't forget to pick me up an order of chicken wings. In spite of what the experts say about fried foods being high in cholesterol and detrimental to our innards, those wings are supposed to be king of the hill and I wouldn't mind sinking my teeth into 'em!"

Placing his trust in both the cat and meat-craving dog, whom he'd tutored to operate as a team, Larry had no doubt that things would be well cared for while he was away. He was also sure if anything needed to be brought to his attention, his conscientious colleagues would get on their horses and promptly alert him. Thus, leaving the animals to free-wheel, Larry discarded his binoculars, traversed the tiki hut's wooden ramp, and trotted toward the north end of Sunset Beach. Like a chameleon, he'd unobtrusively blend with the dispersed crowd of people and would disappear from sight.

Becoming more visible, Beach Cat and Dune Dog put their parked bodies in drive and rose from the ground. After thoroughly stretching their legs, 'THUR-R-R-RIP,' they shook a fine coating of vexing sand from their furry bottoms and moved to the front of the lifeguard station. Customarily, Beach Cat assumed full command. Stringently, he unraveled his strategy. "As always, Dune, we'll divide our territory! This time, I'm staying right here in the middle of the map. For your latitude and longitude, you'd best pull-up a chair somewhere on my north side…preferably diagonal to the cave. If ya want, when Larry passes you on his way back, you can punch-out and head for home. Oh, and before ya go anywhere, get a hold of Peter and tell him to screen the south shore. Even though there ain't much goin' on down there, I'd feel more at ease if he kept it under surveillance."

"Gotcha," complied Dune; "I'm on it!"

Kicking-up gobs of sand with his paws, Dune dodged a number of mobile beach-goers and galloped over to the ocean, where he signaled for a nearby on-the-wing Peter to put an end to his eminent mode of fishing. "RUFF ~ RUFF...Stop - Stop!" barked the retriever. "Get over here, bird-brain," he hollered; "I gotta speak to you!"

Obedient to his page, Peter flew over to the beach and circled low overhead. "What is it, Dune?" he asked. "Whatta ya bothering me for...can't ya see I'm tryin' to find something to eat?!"

Being short about it, Dune downloaded his instructions. "Forget about the early-bird special and put this on your bulletin board! Larry went for a jog and we're relieving him. Beach Cat's taking charge and he wants you to case the south end."

Happy to facilitate his leader and contribute to the cause, Peter put his appetite on the back burner and reciprocated the descriptive canine's lighthearted digs. "Okay, dog-breath," he squawked; "until I hear otherwise, I'm out of the kitchen and in the crow's nest!"

Without further ado, they got on with their individual missions. In contrast to Dune hustling over to his designated land-based post, Peter was climbing high in the sky, rising far above the beach. Strategically, his maneuver would allow him to expand his keen eyesight and concentrate on both the water and shoreline.

Ready to go to work and improve his view as well, Beach Cat scurried up the ramp to the tiki hut and jumped onto the structure's wrap-around porch railing. His new lofty limelight location nurtured his lifeguard sensations. "This is great!" he thought. "I love it when I'm here by myself...it's such a nice place to be...it's so relaxing...and stimulating, too! It also gets a guy a lot of recognition...I can already count one...two...yeah, three people waving hello to me...and I've got a couple of girls smiling at me over there! Yes sir-ree...now all I need is Larry's yellow swimsuit, his vogue hair-do, and to fasten on his guitar and I'll be all set...except I can't play the guitar or sing for anyone...but at least I'd have the ambiance! Boy oh boy," he expressed to himself, "Larry really has it made...and he knows it! And if it wasn't for having to go in the water, I'd cherish taking over his...hey...wait a minute...uh oh...why am I thinking this way? I'm getting carried away again...shame on me!" he muttered. "I've done this job numerous times and I'm still slipping-up! I'd better snap out of it and get on with what I'm supposed to be doing. Nothing's ever happened on my watch and I'm not about to ruin my record!"

Yes sir-ree, as time wore on and austerity displaced the tomcat's complacency, he found it to be the same mind-consuming chore and almost more than he could do to keep tabs on his enthralling surroundings and the menagerie of activities. To his front-side, in the lively ocean, a thinning but still significant integration of adults and children were either swimming, snorkeling, laughing and talking, or riding on floats. Over on dry land, fitted among their parents and the remaining last-ditch sunbathers, diapered toddlers and older preoccupied young-ins were frolicking in the sand. Markedly adding their athletic movements and pulsating beat of their CD-player to the gathering, in their semi-private out-of-the-way niche, a small troop of teenagers were zestfully enjoying their competitive game of volleyball. Concurrently, sandwiched in the thick of things, others were casually strolling or meticulously beachcombing along the water's edge. Some were hoping to find themselves a colorful seashell or two; or maybe even a washed-up and blackened prehistoric shark tooth!

Seemingly lost in their own serene little world, no one ever envisioned Mother Nature's fury eclipsing their weekend respite. In fact, lurking only minutes from shore was a danger that would eventually wreak havoc on the beach! Sensing the threat in its early stages was none other than Peter the pelican.

Unexpectedly, during his south-bound airborne patrol, 'FOOSH,' he was buzzed and nearly had his head taken off by a flock of fast-flying sea gulls, who were fleeing from the ocean with reckless abandonment. At first, an irate and grousing Peter wondered why the gulls had discourteously crossed his flight-path. Once he'd panned the sky, he realized what their actions were all about. "Good night!" he uttered. "Those are some of the darkest clouds I've ever seen!"

Right away, he tilted his wings, turned himself around, and 'SWOOM,' he was flying feverishly, bent on informing Beach Cat of an oncoming storm.

Following his brisk trip, Peter was gasping for air when he landed beside his feline friend back at the lifeguard station. In attempting to convey his gloomy weather report, the winded sea bird's stressed-out sentence sounded like complete gibberish. "THARNK ~ STARNK ~ CARNKA ~ WAW-KA!" he squawked.

"Whoa...calm down, Peter!" quelled Beach Cat. "You're talking in pelican talk...and with me never getting into your native language, you'll have to translate what ya said. Now, tell me what's the matter... what's wrong with you? My guess is that ya mistakenly swallowed a stingray and it's stabbing your insides with its venomous barb! Is that what you're jibber-jabbering about?"

Upon taking a deep breath to compose himself, Peter gestured upward with one of his wings and spoke in understandable terms. "What I'm...I'm tryin' to say is we're about to get hit by a big ol' lightning maker! Its rolling up behind those other clouds...take a gander...its...its pretty scary!"

Dropping his nonchalant attitude, an apprehensive Beach Cat raised his head and eyed the sky. Sure enough, from the southwest, he saw a blossoming storm approaching at high-speed. Automatically, he called on his training. "There's no time to waste!" he bellowed. "We gotta spread the word and get this beach squared-away as soon as possible!"

Handily hanging in the proximity of where the two were sitting on the tiki hut was a rusty eighteenth-century pirate ship bell. Ominously adorned with a skull and cross bones, it was the beach's multi-purpose danger and retreat alarm, which covered any and all hazards from air to sea and was about to be applied. "Peter, start ringing the bell...get everyone out of the water and away from here!" instructed beach Cat. "In the meantime, I'm gonna locate Larry and Dune...I wanna make sure they know what all the noise is about!"

"Alright, no problem!" voiced Peter. "Do what you have to do and I'll get on with delivering the message."

Indeed, after hitching his bill onto the bell's dangling rope, 'CLANG ~ CLANG ~ CLANG,' the pelican sounded a loud warning. Those who understood and respected what they heard, put a fast halt to their activities. Once they'd looked around and discovered what they were in for, at the birth of a strong variable breeze, they gathered their personal possessions and hastily headed for shelter. As they did so, 'CLANG ~ CLANG ~ CLANG,' Peter continued to ring the alarm, hoping that all would take heed and vacate the vicinity.

With the anchored sea bird controlling the southern regions, to the north of him, Beach Cat was in full stride, sprinting along the coast and slinging words of caution to meandering men, women, and children. Sometime later, when he came upon Dune Dog, he was pleased to see that he'd responded to the distant bell and was already placing the people around him on their guard. Now pacing back and forth in the frothy surf, assertively, he was passing the buck. "RUFFA ~ RUFFA ~ RUFFA...Storm - Storm - Storm!" he barked. "Get out of the water!" yelled the dog. "Get yourselves off the beach!"

For his vigilance and right-on jargon, Dune received a commendable nod from a close at hand Beach Cat. Not that it was totally unanticipated, but at that particular phase of their predominantly uneventful groundwork, suddenly, 'WHOOSH,' a heavier wind set-in and the once docile ocean started to boil with high waves! The surly squall's disruptive arrival was more than enough to get everyone up in arms and on the go, including Beach Cat. "I'm leaving, Dune!" he announced. "Stick around and direct the traffic, will ya? If there's any stragglers, I'll be back to help ya get 'em rounded up!"

"Affirmative!" replied the retriever. "Hey, by the way, where ya off to...are ya tryin' to find Larry in Buffalo?"

Shouting on the fly, Beach Cat verified Dune's innuendo. "Yeah... besides remindin' him about your chicken wings, I wanna let him know we're on top of things!"

Whilst the Maine Coon raised his sails and motored-on, Sunset Beach's modest three-mile-long shoreline was gradually being engulfed by the leading edge of the storm, which was wielding an increasing amount of thunderous lightning and beginning to drop a torrential mixture of rain and marble-sized hail. Consequently, people were running, stumbling, and streaming about in every direction! In lieu of recovering their beach paraphernalia, some were high-stepping-it for the refuge of their waterfront homes or nearby parked cars.

The riotous and confusing mass movement of bodies not only brought Beach Cat to an acquiescent standstill, but also made it trying for him to weed-out the lone person he was seeking. "Larry... hey, Larry!" he hollered. "Larry...Larry, talk to me!"

After getting no response, he flagged-down and quizzed a number of recognizable beach-goers, who in their restless passing failed to provide him with any useful information concerning his mentor's whereabouts. Literally turning the other cheek, he canned his land search, pivoted westward, and concentrated on the rough jagged ocean. It wasn't long before he pinpointed Larry and two others floating amongst a host of roller-coaster waves!

Because of the storm's surprise insurrection and resulting repercussions, the lifeguard was obligated to swim to the aid of a young woman and her five-year-old daughter, who were dragged far from shore by a gripping rip current and were unable to make it back to the beach. Presently, in a chain-like out of synch fashion, lead-swimming Larry and the middle-set mother were pulling on the rope of her child's float. Wishing he hadn't gone and done it, Larry was cursing his jog for health! The taxing workout left him dehydrated and almost up the creek without a paddle as he attempted to breast stroke with one arm and his cumbersome tight-muscled legs. Fortunately, he saw a familiar critter standing on the seaboard and cried for assistance, which due to his isolated location was barely discernable. "Yoe, Beach Cat! Get me…get me two life preservers from the hut! Hurry…I'm cramping-up!"

In acknowledgement, Beach Cat did all he could to give the lifeguard a psychological lift. "Keep trucking, Larry!" he shouted. "The floats are on their way!"

Again, the black-striped feline was off to the races. However, this time around, he found himself going against the storm's grain and beset by its fur-parting winds. During his arduous trip toward home base, he connected with his waiting canine cohort. "What's the…what's the word?" asked the laboring Maine Coon. "Is your area secure, Dune?"

"Yeah, everyone's gone!" he replied. "They left all kinds of stuff lying around, but other than that, this sector's clear."

"Good…then your affairs are finished here," voiced Beach Cat. "So make like a bullet and come with me!"

Unaware of the off-shore crisis up the coast, Dune was curious to learn what was next on the calendar. "Hey, what's happening? Where the heck are we going? Into our cave, I hope!"

Wanting to keep things moving, Beach Cat negated his companion's aspirations with an enlightening and rousing rejoinder. "You can toss your thoughts of the cave, Dune! We've got a code-red situation going on…Larry's in the water and we have to get him a couple of life preservers as fast as we can! Peter's at the hut and we'll have him fly them over to save time. While he's in the air, we can transport some dry blankets. Now, let's make hay, before we lose Larry and the people that are with him!"

The bare-bones synopsis was all Dune had to hear. Taking it from there, he filed-in behind Beach Cat and 'SH-R-R-ROOM,' they high-tailed it for the lifeguard station.

Down the sandy road, once the out-of-breath animals arrived at their destination, they discovered their pelican pal was no longer around. "This ain't too promising!" uttered Dune to Beach Cat. "I thought ya…I thought ya said Peter was here."

"Well, he was…he was manning the alarm when I lit-out for you and Larry," replied the puzzled feline. "I wonder where he went? We gotta…we gotta find him!"

Frantically checking high, low, near and far, through an opaque veil of rain and hail, at last, Beach Cat sighted the sea bird. "I see him!" he bellowed. "Yeah, it's Peter alright!"

"WOOF ~ WOOF…Where - Where?" asked Dune.

Pointing with his paw, Beach Cat steered Dune's eyes and consideration in a remote southerly direction, where Peter was fanning his wings over the ocean. In his hooked bill, the shore-minded pelican was grasping a nylon tow rope. Strenuously, he was pulling on a wayward float that was carrying an irresponsible wave-boogeying twelve-year-old boy, who was holding onto the sides of his recreational raft for dear life and was obviously in distress! Plainly, Peter was involved with his own rescue operation and was in no position to lend his usefulness elsewhere. "My, oh my, oh my," mouthed Dune, "there's our answer as to why the bird flew the coop. Dear, John to us…Peter's gonna be tied-up for longer than we'd like!"

"Exactly," muttered a frowning Beach Cat. "Ya know, it's too bad I'm not seeing our high performance speedboat and jet ski in the water anymore…we could really use 'em right now! Dear, John to us again…they're gone…and I don't think we have enough time to switch with Peter. Nahhh…we'd better not try it…it'd be too much of a gamble…we'll have to deal with those floats and take 'em to Larry ourselves!"

Before the duo got back on the hoof, their attention was drawn to the north of Peter, where a blue-colored beach buoy was moored close to shore. Fine tuning their sensitive hearing, an ear-twitching Dune and Beach Cat were homing in on a prevailing noise that was growing louder and louder!

As they looked-on and listened from the realm of the tiki hut, they saw two funnel-shaped silhouettes appear below a thick bank of greenish-black clouds. Eerily, the shadowy objects began to spiral downward. Upon linking with the energized ocean, 'F-R-R-ROOM,' they transformed into small but potent waterspouts! Quickly, they gathered momentum, sucked-up the weighty buoy marker, and moved eastward, which put them dead on with the gawking dog and cat.

Stupefied by the funnels' evolution and petrified by their approach, 'GULP,' Dune swallowed hard, clenched his paws for traction, and prior to ogling Beach Cat for feedback, he accentuated the matter at hand. "Gadzooks! Talk about killer vacuum cleaners…they must be the real expensive high-powered models…no bag required…and only one swipe necessary!"

"You've got them pegged," said Beach Cat. "They're the kind that'll suck the rug right off your floor and out through the chimney… it tells me that we have to speed it up! C'mon, Dune…we gotta get in the hut and on our way before those vacuum cleaners take us and everything else with them!"

Just as they were about to scramble, they watched the unpredictable waterspouts go with the wind and veer away. To the animals' relief, they were moving northward. Unfortunately, their new course posed a threat to lifeguard Larry and the people under his care. The change in developments didn't go unnoticed. "We've been given a big reprieve, Dune!" bellowed Beach Cat. "But who can say about Larry…what's in store for him? Shiver me timbers…how many more complications are we gonna have?! It's beginning to make me think that instead of obeying Larry and comin' back to the hut, I should've stayed where I was at and joined him in the water. But it's not what he wanted from me…and my speculating isn't doing us any good. That's why we'd best tend to Larry before we have another bombshell dropped on us…him too!"

"I'm on your tail, Beach Cat!" assured Dune. "Let's forget about those body wraps and just get the essentials!"

Summarily, they entered the hut, bypassed a stack of plastic-sealed blankets, and lunged at a pair of tubular-shaped life preservers. With the tow lines to the yellow-colored floats firmly fixed in their teeth, they made their exit and zipped along the beach!

In the interim, as his furry friends grew tired from running and dragging their flip-flopping rescue equipment, Larry was steadily weakening from towing his arm-wrenching mother and child load. After being pushed further from land by a recurring rip current, the threesome's situation was about to take another turn for the worse when unexpectedly, 'WHAM - SPLASH,' they were hit broadside by an immense wave! Abruptly, its sheer brute force separated the little girl from Larry and her mother. Although the battered five-year-old was still seated in her chair-like pontooned float, she was swiftly stolen away by the high swells and more unfavorable out-going currents. "Mommy…mommy!" she screamed. "Mommy…where are you? I'm scared…I'm scared! Where are you?"

When the horrified mother saw her curly-haired offspring floating away, she totally fell to pieces. "My baby…my baby!" she hollered. "I have to get my baby!"

Vigorously, she tugged and fought to free her arrested wrist from Larry's tight grip. "Let go of me!" she begged. "Please…let me go after my daughter!"

"No…no!" shouted Larry. "I'm sorry, I…I can't let ya do it…I can't let ya go after her! It's for your own good…now stop pulling away from me!"

Sadly, an experienced and lucid Larry was all too aware that nothing immediate could be done for the hapless youngster. He knew that as long as she remained strapped to her high-tech float and was able to avoid the zigzagging waterspouts he'd spied, she'd have a reasonable possibility of staying alive. He also knew it wouldn't be kosher to unhand the girl's hysterical and well-drawn mother, for without a life preserver, she'd most likely drown!

Persecuted by his problematic limitations, Larry felt terrible and was at a complete loss for words as the desperate woman continued to grapple with him. "I said, let go of me!" she demanded. "I have to get my daughter! My poor baby...my little Emma...I don't wanna live without my baby...God, help me...please...help me!"

Coincidentally, shortly after the wave did its damage, both a heavily-panting Dune Dog and Beach Cat arrived along the distant and now totally deserted shoreline. Once he'd scanned the ocean and deliberated on the situation, Beach Cat placed the tether to his life preserver in front of his ninety-pound assistant and gave him an order. "Here, Dune, take my float with ya out to...out to Larry and the woman!"

Baffled by the Maine Coon's actions, Dune spit his tow rope on the ground and sought an explanation. "I don't get it...I know ya...ya hate goin' in the water...its no secret! It never stopped ya before though...so, why aren't you coming with me? Whatta ya planning on doing...writing your...your memoirs or what?"

Catering to Dune's audacious query, Beach Cat motioned toward a faint red-colored downstream float, which still had its adolescent owner aboard and was drifting off to the northwest. "I'm goin' for that little girl," he replied. "At least I think it's a girl! At one point, she was with Larry. Evidently, something went haywire...therefore, we have to split-up!"

Searching for the detached third-person in question, Dune re-examined the ocean and spotted a small child, who appeared to be on an intersecting tract with the feared waterspouts. Figuring it would take monumental measures and the participation of a superlative being to save her, he put a temporary hold on things. "WARF ~ WARF...Wait - Wait!" he barked. "Before you do anything, Beach Cat, you should talk to the Wisdom and ask for help! If you're gonna have any chance at all of pulling off that long-swim rescue, I'd say you'll need it...more so than ever if you have a rumble with those funnels! And just for the record," voiced the dog, "I'm not a spring chicken anymore...and because of the heavy seas and all the back-breaking swimming I've gotta do, you just might have to use the donations and boost you'll get from the 'Big Guy' to salvage what's left of me!"

Pitting his hindsight against the retriever's foresight, Beach Cat touched on a stipulation which generally governed his defensive lightning and other abilities that were periodically granted to him by the Wisdom of the Orange. "Dune, what you're saying is for me to place the wagon ahead of the horse, and I can't do it! If you recall, the Wisdom's spirit is always watching and judging my actions...and determining my needs. In this particular case, I know from past experience that unless I'm willing to put my best to the test, which I've yet to do by taking on that rescue, then I wouldn't even get the time of day from the Wisdom. Its the bottom line! Another bottom line goes like this...later on, if I were to ask the Wisdom for help out there in the water and didn't try hard enough to earn it, then other than for myself, it could end up spelling real trouble for you if you're depending on me...understand?"

"Hey, I'm not lookin' to invite more trouble than what we've already got!" retorted Dune. "I'm also not gonna squabble with you about the fine print restrictions you have in your contract with the Wisdom! I just thought it would be nice if there was an overlooked loophole that would allow you to skip the preliminary do-it-yourself stuff and give us a head-start on what we're going up against."

"Yeah, well, the head-start is us!" emphasized Beach Cat. "And there's no getting around the Wisdom's standards...they're set in stone. Now, grab those floats and let's get cracking...we gotta put some muscle into this!"

Answering their macho call to glory, gingerly, they stepped into the briny drink, got a feel for their surroundings, and went their separate ways.

Shortly thereafter, upon treading through relentless rows of high waves, Dune eventually reached his objective. Fluidly, he passed his two floats over to the sobbing mother and an appreciative Larry. "Thanks, Dune...thanks a...thanks a bunch!" gasped the lifeguard. "My legs are stiffer than stale bread and I needed this break! Plus, with rip currents and those...those funnels springing-up, its turned into a bees nest out here...that makes you none too soon in your arrival! You're quite the St. Bernard, aren't ya?!"

Dune snorted a snootful of stinging water from his nostrils and promptly returned Larry's courtesy, admonishing him to boot. "Son,

I'm glad to be of service…only I'm not a St. Bernard…I'm a Golden Retriever!"

After chalking one up for his heritage, the fatigued animal started swimming into deeper northwest waters. His seemingly errant impulse was scrutinized by Larry, who hollered in befuddlement. "Yoe, Dune…check your compass…the shore's back this way! Do ya realize what you're doing?"

"You're fussin' for nothing!" replied the head-turning dog. "I know exactly what I'm doing! I'm looking for Beach Cat…he's trying to save a little girl on a red float. If I can…can find him in all these waves, I'm gonna help him!"

As the missing child's mother lackadaisically embraced her life preserver, her reaction to Dune's come-back reeked of pessimism. "My baby's gone!" she moaned. "I lost her…I lost my daughter."

Refusing to throw in the towel, Dune offered the woman a glimmer of hope, which centered on his feline commander in chief. "Lady, no one's gonna be…gonna be gone with my friend, Beach Cat around. Take it from me, he's got something up his sleeve that can…can make a difference!"

Integrating what the dog was alluding to, a supportive Larry begrudgingly surrendered to what was eating at his rescue procedure intellect and cagily proffered his best wishes to his ambitious students. "Good-luck to both of you, Dune…you can do it! Show me your savvy…show me what ya got! Just be…just be careful…these waters are the pits…it's why I sent Beach Cat for the floats! And I don't care if he's…if he's got the Wisdom up his sleeve or not…he shouldn't be off by himself! You shouldn't be alone either…it's bad protocol! So, watch yourself…cuzz you won't have me to look after ya…and beware of rip currents…there could be more of 'em!"

On those parting remarks, Larry dipped into his energy reserves and pulled the grief-stricken mother toward shore while Dune kept his previous heading.

Simultaneously, somewhere in the wild and wooly yonder, equating with the others, Beach Cat was literally taking it on the chin from the turbulent seas and strong face-lashing winds. Albeit that he'd made up a lot of ground in his agonizing pursuit of the girl, inevitably, from what he'd noted, the unyielding side-door waterspouts had an edge on him and would be first to encroach upon and possibly have a go at her. Adding to his woes, while bobbing up and down, he saw Emma and her float getting whacked, flipped, and snowed under by an insurgent wave!

Following her swallowing a mouthful of choking salt water, Emma popped to the ocean's surface right-side-up, wiped her burning eyes, and cried for her guardian. "Mommy...'Cough ~ Cough'...mommy... mommy...I can't hear you...where are you? Mommy...'Cough ~ Cough'...mommy...help me-e-e-e!"

The beseeching youngster's dreadful dilemma caused Beach Cat to sink into absolute despair. In relation to the circumstances, instinctively, he recalled what the Wisdom of the Orange had told him on his consecration day. "Evil and earthly devices you are not to fear!" said God. "When you find yourself in danger or mired in dismay, in order to draw on your uplifting strength and other powers, you'll have to pray!"

Amidst his mental, physical, and opportune fight to stay afloat, the Maine Coon requested support by reeling-off an invaluable simplistic verse, one that he learned to respect the hard way. "Eternal Wisdom!" he shouted. "In my weak...dark...and...and yearning hour...give me courage and stability...if necessary...bestow upon me your...your supremacy...amen!"

Low and behold, Beach Cat's 'S.O.S.' had been heard by the invisible Wisdom. From the milieu of the animal's disturbed soul, God spoke his peace. **"My little angel, do not give up...hold your head high! At this time, you must remain patient and keep moving, for your water-bound venture forbids the growth of your claws and the safe use of your resourceful lightning. Even so, what I'm about to entrust to you will not only be encouraging, but will also award to you whatever my interacting spirit has surmised to be worthy and mandatory! Last of all,"** said the Almighty, **"if you're burden ever becomes too heavy and my earthly division sanctions it, in your deprived time, I promise to be there dutifully! Thus, carry on with your good works and resume your journey."**

Suddenly, waking up was the dormant citrus juice that Beach Cat consumed years ago. With the tingling heavenly substance actively coursing through his veins and conductive nerve endings,

'BA-ZOOM,' his former lackluster eyes took on a florescent-orange glow! In turn, his compliant body flinched, shuttered, distended and doubled in mass. Despite his claws remaining at par and devoid of their supercharged clout of energy, still, he could feel the rejuvenating strength and courage of a tiger stewing inside of him!

All at once, 'SWISH~ SWISH ~ SWISH,' Beach Cat picked-up the cadence to his swimming. The more little Emma screamed for help, the more he chugged his paws and the faster he swam! Yet, that alone wouldn't be enough to get 'er done. Ergo, as an essential Wisdomatic bonus, Beach Cat received a big shove on his submerged tush from a gully-washing rip current, which sent him bodysurfing and en route for Emma! Before the oceanic river of water came to a crest and expended itself, it boosted and consigned him well within her range. Resting on his laurels, he relayed to her a staunch guarantee. "Hold on, girlie…I'm…I'm comin' for ya…I'm comin' to get ya!"

Demonstrating his sincerity and pumped-up physical prowess, he surged ahead, and with his sharp teeth, he grabbed onto the ten-foot long rope that was attached to Emma's float. Now that he'd beaten the nearby waterspouts to the draw, sharply, he reversed his field and took his precious five-year-old cargo in tow.

Giving it his all, the dogpaddling feline was making a valiant attempt to swim to safety. However, after traveling a good stone's throw and peering over his shoulder, he saw the funnels had altered their direction and were currently shadowing him. Slowly but surely, 'WUR-R-R-R-R,' their rumbling low-pitched roar was becoming more profound!

Auspiciously, because of his contact with the tried and true Wisdom, Beach Cat didn't feel the least bit threatened by the raging compound storm. In fact, he felt well-protected and knew it was only a matter of time before his nose-to-the-grindstone works would bear him more fruit.

His wait for something wondrous to happen would be negligible, for out of the blue, by means of God's guidance, 'SPLASH'…"URFF," Dune Dog appeared among the clashing waves. Advantageously, they shook, rattled, heaved and deposited him alongside an ecstatic Beach Cat, who had a mouthful of rope and consequently, a real problem with pronouncing some of his words. "Hoe-wee cow…it's…it's good

28

to see ya, buddy…I'm gwad ya could make it! It sure is wavy and wuff out here, isn't it?!"

"Yep-per, it's…it's rough alright!" confirmed Dune. "There's… there's rip currents too…I was just given a ride by one! It may be a…a tad late for this, Beach Cat," he uttered, "but the next time we think about taking one of these cheap cut-rate cruises, we should…should upgrade our itinerary and…and get ourselves a boat with the deal! Seriously though, concerning upgrades, I can…I can tell by your eyes and big ol' body that you've been…been talking to the Wisdom! So what's the scoop…how come you haven't sprung your claws and used your…your lightning to do away with those waterspouts? You'd better make 'em disappear before they do the same to us!"

Putting things in their proper perspective, an antsy speech-impaired Beach Cat flung his head sideways and offered part of the float's towline to his floppy-eared companion. "Here, Dune, I want ya to…to gwab onto that wope and start swimming! In other words, I'm saying I don't have my power-bolts…they can't be used in these conditions. Now, wet's…wet's get going!"

Once he'd caught wind of the bad news, dog-tired ten-year-old Dune took another look at what was spinning toward him and 'ROOSH,' his flattened neck hair stood straight into the air. "You don't have your weapons?!" hollered the gray-chinned canine. "Talk about losing our…our key to success, I don't think we're gonna make it…those funnels are almost on us, and I'm just about outta gas! Man, I hate to say it, Beach Cat, but right now, I wish we were…were Fred and Charlie. Those bums are in the cave unwinding while we're putting our lives on the line! If anything, that lazy Fred could be…could be sashaying all of us into shore! And that wimpy little Charlie…for the love of Mike, all he's ever good for is litter and glass patrol! Ya know, it doesn't seem fair that we're…we're gettin' stuck with the…the short end of the stick…and since we are…then like ya said…we'd b-b-better get going!"

Propelled by a huge rush of adrenaline, Dune took hold of the float's towline, aligned himself eastward, and from his vanguard position, he swam for his salvation! Along the way, he and Beach Cat continued to count on Larry's coaching, which in part, involved taking frequent breaths of air and synchronizing their leg movements to stave off fatigue. Waste not want not, they'd also brought their lengthy flexible tails into their scheme of escape, using them as rudders to help them navigate through the ruthless current and white-capped waves.

For all their abetting ingenuity and the impressive head of steam they'd generated, disappointingly, as they brought Emma past the midway point to land, behind them, 'WUR-R-R-R,' the noisy funnels were still clawing at their heels!

Rising to the occasion, from his backseat location, Beach Cat tried to keep his nervous driver's fragile spirits from shattering. "You're doin' weal good, Dune," he muttered; "you've got us on…on easy stweet…we don't have far to go. Just keep concen-twating on the beach ahead of us…and don't make any wong turns!"

While tendering an answer through his occupied mouth, Dune got himself a taste of the tomcat's scrambled vocabulary. "Easy stweet isn't good enough for me!" he gurgled. "I'm wooking for the on-wamp to the thwu-way…we should be weaching it soon!"

Speaking of weaching, or reaching that is, without warning, a human hand shot out of the water and 'WHAP,' it grabbed onto a loose piece of towline that was wafting in front of the Golden Retriever's face. Startled by the disturbance, "YIKES," Dune yelped, put on the brakes, and dropped his designated portion of the rope!

When the individual who was attached to the fisted hand surfaced for air, Dune warbled in astonishment. "Whoa…Larry!" he gasped. "It's you…ya came after us! How'd ya…how'd ya get here so fast?"

"Hey, I didn't…didn't ace the Olympics by sloughing-off when the crunch was on!" replied the winded lifeguard. "Moreover, the cramps in my legs miraculously disappeared…and providing I don't have a relapse, I'm ready to rock! From what I'm…I'm seeing, I think I know the score…and instead of me messin' around asking useless questions, why don't we…we grind-it-out and give the…the waterspouts a run for their money! Are you guys game or what?!"

Elated to be in the company of one of the world's cream of the crop swimmers, both the submissive dog and an idle on-looking Beach Cat could hardly contain themselves. "We'll do whatever ya say, Larry!" voiced Dune. "You've got the wheel and I'm back on the rope."

"Yeah, you're the man, Lare-wee!" concurred the mush-mouthed Maine Coon. "We'll twy to...twy to keep pace with you!"

Emulating his animal friends' rescue technique, Larry placed the end of the float's knotted towline in his mouth and seized it with his pearly-white teeth. Having the luxury of his arms unfettered and the empowering thrust of eight rearward paws to eliminate drag and improve his efficiency, gradually, one stroke after another, he swam himself into a placid and poised wave-conquering rhythm. And then, 'SPLASH ~ SPLASH ~ SPLASH,' he erupted into a limb-flailing frenzy. His putting the pedal to the metal not only made things more cushy for Beach Cat and Dune Dog, but also nearly lifted the toiling twosome half-way out of the ocean!

In short order, their combined efforts enabled them to cover an extensive span and pull Emma away from the 'mysterious-acting' and somewhat distant waterspouts. When their grueling swim was over, they came to rest in shallow water, where Emma's mother was anxiously waiting for them. Lickety-split, she released her unsettled daughter from her float's harness and raised her high into her arms. "My baby!" she cried. "I have my baby girl back! I love you, Emma... I love you lots and lots and lots! I'm so happy to see you...are you okay...are you all right...are ya hurt anywhere?"

"My...my throat hurts a little, mommy," whined Emma. "I'm scared, too! Can we go home now? I wanna go home...please...take me home!"

"Soon, baby...I'll take ya home real soon!" replied her relieved mother. "We have to find my purse and our other belongings on the beach and then we'll go...for now though, I just wanna hold you...I wanna keep you close to me!"

Successive to him conceding a brief but precious allowance for the family reunion celebration, Larry retrieved Emma's float from the murky surf and led everyone onto the southern edge of Treasure Island Beach, which bordered Sunset Beach and was their new setting after having been displaced by the storm. Once ashore, Dune Dog and Beach Cat separated themselves from the pack and 'THUR-R-RAP,' they shook an excess of salt water from their fur. As they stood in place and were being bathed by the diminishing and much more tolerable hail-free rain, they flexed their taut-muscled mouths and focused their attention back on the ocean-born cyclones. "Geeze…can ya believe it, Dune?" remarked Beach Cat. "At first, those waterspouts were bird-dogging us! Right after Larry came up from Neptune's tomb to give us a shot in the arm, I saw them circle each other and trail off from us. Now, they're starting to come at us again! From their mannerism, I'd say the Wisdom definitely put them in gridlock until we could make our get-away. Yes indeed…it was a great feat and one for the archives, wasn't it?"

"G-R-R-R…I don't know…there's something weird about those funnels, Beach Cat!" cautioned the growling retriever. "You can attribute their actions to the Wisdom if ya want…it wouldn't be out of the question. To me though, off the top of my head, it seems as if they're taunting us! I know it's not possible, but it's almost as if they have some sort of intelligence to them. Just looking at them gives me the creeps!"

Getting goose-bumps from ogling one of the conversing animals was an aching, jaw-rubbing, and leg-stretching lifeguard Larry. Like Dune Dog, he'd been long aware of Beach Cat's communication with the Wisdom. Hounded by something on his mind and hard-pressed by a fleeting chance to crusade it, Larry strutted over and planted his shriveled feet in front of the imposing thirty-pound orange-eyed feline. Akin to Dune's prior mention, he was yearning for decisive action. "Hey, Beach Cat," he uttered; "I figured it was too dangerous for you to use your power-bolts in the water, so I didn't bother to ask you about 'em. But with us being on land and not havin' to worry about getting electrocuted, then why don't ya turn on the switch and put those funnels in their place? I don't mean to be uh…to be pushy or anything, but I'd love to see ya heat 'em up and vaporize 'em with your lightning! Yeah, go ahead…give it to 'em good…and while you're at it, you can sweep the sky and disintegrate all their feeder clouds in this area!"

Upon raising one of his front paws and showing off his short claws, for the second time, the Maine Coon divulged his limitations. "Larry, you can forget about my weapons coming into play! Just as you thought, I couldn't use 'em in the ocean…the Wisdom wouldn't even let me have 'em. And now that we're away from the waterspouts, I doubt I'll be needing 'em. If they were necessary, I'm positive they'd be permitted! On the flip side of that coin, until this storm blows over and life gets back to normal, I'm gonna keep the power that was allotted to me for insurance purposes. Who knows, if something unforeseeable arises, it might come in handy!"

"Well, Beach Cat," lipped Larry, "I'm not gonna argue with God...er uh...I mean the Wisdom over what he wants you to do. I guess he knows best about everything, especially when it comes to you deploying those big guns of yours! However, as I'm sure you're aware of, those funnels are bearing down on us...and if you can't do anything about 'em, then we gotta find some shelter before they get too close!"

A primed Johnny-on-the-spot Dune Dog already had plans made for his parties' next move. "Let's head for the cave, Larry!" he coaxed. "It's a bit of a jaunt for us, but there's no better shelter around for this type of storm...we'll ride-out what's left of it in there. To cover all the bases and avoid any tragedies, we'll take the child and her mother with us. Yeah, fetch 'em over here before they wander into harm's way and let's get rolling!"

In compliance to the canine's directive, persuasively, Larry collected the gals, and through the persistent rain, everyone retreated from Treasure Island and the 'danger zone' where they'd been loitering. Taking the path of least resistance, they hugged the shoreline and scooted along its smooth water-packed surface.

Once they'd crossed boundaries and beat thousands of feet onto Sunset Beach, they angled eastward and passed by a tall thicket of sea oat plants that were encompassing and providing cover for a small cemetery. Years back, the private burial ground was founded by the cave-dwellers. It was where they'd paid their last respects and laid to rest a number of by-gone beach critters; many of whom they'd known and many they didn't. In remembrance and without prejudice, they thoughtfully marked each and every one of the hallowed gravesites with an ornamental sea shell. At some time in the future, when their individual clocks ticked their last, they all intended on being buried and having a diminutive monument of their own in the seaside bone-yard!

Continuing onward, the waterlogged group weaved through an assorted-sized cluster of palm trees and approached their rocky refuge, which tunneled into the base of the largest of the beach's multiple in-line sand dunes. On their arrival, they were met by both a yawning Fred the turtle and Charlie the crab. Barely awake from their earlier nap, they'd left the moderate seventy-five-degree confines of the cave, and from an elevated clearing in the trees, they happened to observe the latter part of their harried friends' action-packed performance.

Teasingly expressing his outlook concerning the rescue operation, Charlie proceeded to poke fun at Larry, Dune, and a reconstructed Beach Cat, who were flanking little Emma and her security-minded mother. "You guys seem to be in an awfully big hurry!" he stressed with a provocative grin. "Is there a problem? Hey, wait a second… don't tell me…I think I know! All of you have to go to the bathroom, so Beach Cat said his prayer and asked the Wisdom for some extra vitality to help him double-time everyone into shore, right? Nahhh… that can't be it…how dumb of me…ya could've gone to the bathroom in the water! Let me see here…maybe uh…maybe you're in a hurry because y'all heard about the day-long yard sale they're havin' over at the condo complex behind the cave…is that it?"

Piling-on to Charlie's witty creativity, Fred boldly went for the gusto. "Yard sales and piddling in the ocean are trivial compared to what's on my mind!" he hollered. "In the name of mutinous naughtiness…how many times do I have to tell you kids not to play with waterspouts?! Hmmm…you won't like this, but for misbehaving, I want all of you to go to your rooms and stay there until your father gets home from work…that's when you're really gonna get it!"

Despite the fact Fred and Charlie were just being their typical selves, their indifferent cohorts were in no mood for any nonsense; Dune Dog in particular. "G-R-R-RUFF…knock it off!" he barked. "For your information, you guys, I don't take kindly to your mouthy monkey business…it's tacky in front of our company! And talk about fodder for disrespectful folly," denoted the dog, "I could easily pick on you over that painful-looking sunburn of yours. As much as you deserve it, I'm not gonna lay it on thick about your charred carcasses. But in reference to who's been misbehaving, Fred, I'd advise you and Charlie to clean up your act…or you'll find me sending ya back to the Bahamas…for good!"

"Yeah, if you two can somehow put a lid on your wisecracks," added Beach Cat, "we'd like to get out of this weather and inside the cave…where it's safe!"

Feeling slighted himself, Larry took advantage of the opportunity to get even with the clowning turtle and crab. "Look here, dudes!" he summoned. "To make up for the excitement ya missed, maybe you should go and give those waterspouts a scenic tour of the beach towns! It would be the considerate thing to do…don't ya think?"

Larry's resentful suggestion was unequivocally declined. "Lawson, what I'm thinkin' is you must be delirious from overexertion!" said Fred. "I'm no travel guide…and I ain't about to become one."

"I'm with you, Fred," sustained Charlie. "At the prospect of me ruining my 'nice guy' reputation by being inhospitable, I wouldn't wanna show those waterspouts anything…except for how to leave the building!"

Now that everyone was on the same page, they all entered the protective, down-sloping, and for the moment, quite noisy cave. Judgmentally, once Dune Dog had gotten Emma and her mother situated, he sought to rectify the ruckus problem by imparting his protest to a stylishly gyrating Fred and an ungainly-looking Charlie, who were prominently bee-bopping around the stony perimeter of their thirty-square-foot pond. "Alright, you dingledorff squires…hear ye` - hear ye`…this is your lord and master talking, and I want ya to stop your dancing and turn my stereo off! Its too loud and I'm sick and tired of havin' to put-up with your screechy music. It gives me high blood-pressure and drives me nuts! I want it peaceful and sane in here…ya got it?"

"Okay, Dune," said Fred, "you'll get your sanity back…in a couple of minutes or less. Right now, my favorite song, 'Big Fat Ugly Toe' is playing…and if you can be civil about it, we'll just wait until its over before we turn the radio off."

"No we won't!" retorted an emphatic Dune. "We're not waiting for anything…and don't give me none of your civil dribble…just put a muzzle on your maniacal tunes!"

Unlike his procrastinating turtle friend, an on-the-crawl and somewhat sarcastic Charlie was more than happy to satisfy the canine's demand. "I never did care much for this hokey song from the day it made its debut!" he announced. "Its herky-jerky tempo makes it hard for me to keep all of my legs in step with it, and it'd be impossible for it to ever break into the top ten on the C-D charts. For the sake of that, I'll deep-six-it!"

Fred didn't appreciate his other-half's traitorous conduct and vowed for future revenge. "Next time, Charlie, when that 'Warty Nose' song that ya love comes on, I'm gonna deep-six-it on you! How does that grab ya?!"

"Go right ahead!" encouraged the claw-waving crab. "Be my guest, Fred…just don't ever do it when I'm around or I'll filet your chunky body and throw it to the Bull Sharks…with a dab of hot sauce and guacamole! OOOH baby…they'd find that pretty yummy… wouldn't ya say?! How about it, Fred…wouldn't ya say?! Well… aren't you uh…aren't ya gonna answer me? What's…what's up with you…cat got your tongue or something? Are ya really afraid I'm gonna slice and dice ya? Hey…what's with the cold look you're givin' me, Fred? Answer me, will ya? You big cry-baby…answer me! Gosh darn-it…I don't have time for your sulking or immaturity…I'm finished talking to you! I'm finished listening to your song, too…so brace yourself!"

Peeved but swaggering over the silent treatment he was getting from flustered Fred, hasty Charlie made it his aspiration to squelch the radio at the rear of the cave. His esteemed undertaking allowed his weary up-front companions to rest more comfortably. As they did so, Dune Dog reclined on his haunches and exuded an extended sigh as he recounted his side of the story to an adjacent Larry and Beach Cat. "Pheeeeew-Wee…it sure was a close call getting away from those funnels! In all honesty, when I saw 'em comin' at me, I did go to the bathroom in the water! Plus, I thought I was a goner, and I was thinking that after all these years, I never bothered to make out a Will…and then, it struck me…I don't have much to bequeath to anyone anyway. If it came down to it, I figured Charlie and Fred would take possession of my stereo and that would just about liquidate my estate…unless of course they wanted my hairy blanket and food bowl to go along with it!"

While squatting next to Emma's float, Larry drank from a fresh bottle of water which he'd sequestered from the litter left on the beach, wiped his wet brow and classily patronized Dune's legal-matter summation. "I'm another one who never bothered to draw-up any sort of last Will and Testament," he announced. "The footnote to me not having the paperwork to disperse my used goods is…who gives a hoot?! What's more important is that when our chips were down out there, we implemented our own brand of 'will-power' and it paid dividends for us. Yeah, there's nothing like determination and good old coordinated teamwork…it was a job well done, gentlemen! And before I forget…just don't try any more remote rescues without me as a co-pilot…it gets me worried and all teed-off when I see ya violating my regulations!"

Pining to submit his version of things, Beach Cat wasn't about to pull any punches either. From his ground-bound location, he rolled on his side, looked up at Larry, and articulated on his not-so-easy way of making a living. "Hey, man…I know ya love your profession and I'm not about to undermine your training or praising us…or even call ya crazy for what ya do…but if I was ever given the option, I'd never choose to be a full-time open-water lifeguard! That ocean takes a lot out of ya, and it's far too big of a swimming pool for me to ever wanna tangle with on a regular basis. Hopefully, it'll be years before I have to do another mile-long lap in it! To recover from that, I think I'll get together with our nemesis, Jake the landscaper and talk him into letting me keep watch over his outdoor Jacuzzi for a week or two. I'm sure I'll get razzed about it, but it should do me just right. If it doesn't, then I might have to find a stunt double to fill-in for me whenever I'm required to go in the water…or, I could always have a beach-goer call the Coast Guard in Tampa and have them dispatch a rescue helicopter over here…which is what I should've done today!"

After turning away from an indulgent and smiling Larry, the Maine Coon placed his eyes and quizzical thoughts on someone who was once the sole object of his attention. "I realize I'm not the only one who got run through the mill, girlie," he uttered. "I'm sorry it took me so long to get to you! So, how ya doin'…are ya still scared…do ya still wanna go home? Is your throat still sore…should we take ya to a doctor?"

Compassionately, Beach Cat wished to rehash certain particulars and trade small talk with Emma, who presently had her face buried against her mother's bosom and was far too tired and traumatized to speak.

Obligingly, as she sat with her back to one of the cave's side walls and snuggled with her repressed sibling, Emma's emotional teary-eyed mother responded to Beach Cat's rapid-fire inquisition. "I think my...my baby's gonna be just fine!" she proclaimed. "In a sense, it's funny you mentioned taking her to a doctor...it's something I'll be doing once this storm passes. It also seems to be what I've been doing ever since she was born! Yeah, some of you may or may not have noticed, but Emma's had her struggles in life...more than anyone would think for someone her age. However, regardless of what she's had to endure, I can assure you, she's a real fighter...and survivor! I can truly attest to that...especially after this latest ordeal, which almost seemed surreal and caused me to have my doubts about her. I can't explain it, but somehow, she's always managed to pull through the worst of times. I guess...I guess there must be a reason for it. Maybe someday, I'll find out why. Anyhow, I'd like to thank you guys for saving us and bringing my daughter back to me! Ya know, we uh...we just moved into a small apartment in the area and I've been hearing a lot of good things about a lifeguard on this beach and some special animals who live in a cave down here. Obviously, you're the ones I've heard about...and although this wasn't the best way to get acquainted, I'm sure glad you were able to help us and I can't praise you enough for...for taking care of Emma. My little girl means the world to me, and after all we've been through together, I just...I just couldn't imagine...couldn't imagine losing..."

Unable to complete her sentence, the young woman was now openly weeping and shedding tears of joy as she lovingly rocked and warmed her child. Such a heartrending scene spawned awkward feelings amongst the two females' captive man and animal audience. Subsequently, as a mute and somewhat timid Larry walked over to gently place a caring hand on the mother's shoulder, an ill-at-ease Charlie, Fred, and Dune found themselves fidgeting about and exchanging sheepish glances with one another. Joining the club, Beach Cat was up and nervously pacing to and fro, correspondingly canvassing everyone in the cave. Just then, it dawned upon him... 'someone' was missing, which he questioned with great concern. "Hey, you guys...where's Peter? Did ya see him around at all? I'm worried about him...where the heck is he?"

Before giving anyone a chance to reply, 'SH-R-R-ROOM,' he darted from the cave, climbed atop a neighboring sand dune, and from his unobstructed vantage point, he systematically scanned Peter's last known location. Way short of that, in the desolate district of Larry's lifeguard station, he spotted the pelican lying spread-eagle on the ground!

To Peter's credit, the stray wave-boogeying youngster, whom he'd rendered assistance to earlier had long scurried safely home. To Peter's debit, beyond straining his wing muscles, he was virtually spent from pulling on the boy's float and wasn't in a rush to reallocate or undertake any extra curricular activity.

Alarmingly, only a meager half-mile north of the stalled sea bird and just about athwart from where he, himself was sitting, an orange-eyed Beach Cat saw something that sent a fur-raising jolt of electricity along the curvature of his spine...it was the waterspouts! Having been carried southward by an entrapping backpedaling stream of air, they were finally whirling their way onto shore.

Seconds later, once they were fully out of the water, 'WUR-R-ROOSH,' they developed into narrow-bodied hard-core tornados. Ominously, in single-file fashion, they slithered in the direction of an unmindful Peter.

For an on-looking and conscious Beach Cat, a new chapter in the prior epic drama had just begun. "Uh oh!" he muttered. "This doesn't look good...here we go again!"

Setting his peepers back on the pelican, he revved-up his paws and careened down the sand dune, leaving those at the cave to provisionally ponder what he was doing.

Swiftly, he pounded the beach and managed to race and steer ahead of the slower-moving funnel clouds. Behind him, a variety of abandoned lounge chairs, blankets, and large sun-shielding umbrellas were being sucked into the air and confiscated by the long-armed grasp of the tenacious twisters. Giving as well as taking, from their lower-velocity upper winds spewed a mixed bag of water, sand, squiggling live fish and 'KA-ROOM ~ KA-BLAM,' streaks of deadly lightning!

Spurred-on by both his companion's plight and the loud thunderbolts, Beach Cat shifted his legs into high gear and began to move faster than a cheetah. Beneath him, the ground became just a blur as he drew closer and closer to his feathery fixation. Forty feet… thirty feet…twenty feet…ten feet and 'THUMP,' his paws rammed deep into the collapsing weather-beaten remnants of a child-made sand castle. Near to where he stopped was an indolent Peter, who after seeing the huffing and puffing feline standing on his doorstep, raised his previously-sagging head and started a rather energetic conversation. "Leapin' lizards, Beach Cat! Where did you come from? You've been gone for quite a while…whatta ya been up to?"

"Other than tryin' to corral you," said the Maine Coon, "I was…I was busy helping Larry and a little girl…she and her mother are in the cave with the rest of the bunch. But never mind about what I've been up to! Before we vamoose from here, Peter, what I'd…I'd like to know from you is what happened to the kid in the water that Dune and I saw ya towing…is he…is he on land?"

"Yeah, he's on land," responded the pelican. "I'll go so far as to say he's probably on his way out of town!"

"Good show," extolled Beach Cat; "that's kudos for you, Peter! Now, let's get ourselves inside the cave…it's where we oughtta be. Trust me, this is no time to be dilly-dallying around! If you look down the shoreline, you'll see a couple of tornados on the prowl…and unless you wanna be sucked-up and torn apart, you'd better get off your duff, make like a jet, and fly hard!"

Throttled by exhaustion and wracked with pain, Peter morosely shunned Beach Cat's advice, insightfully putting it to task. "How am I supposed to fly?" he carped. "It's too windy out here…and with the shape my wings are in, they'd never get me over to the cave. To be blunt with ya, I'm not goin' anywhere…unless it's to the animal emergency room…in an ambulance!"

Synonymous to what Dune, Larry and his other amigos perceived earlier, Peter saw the pronounced larger-than-life changes in someone's persona and vehemently tacked-on his high expectations. "For crying out loud, Beach Cat…cancel the ambulance, we've got the Wisdom on our side! So whatta ya comin' unglued about? All ya have to do is turn your weapons on those tornados and get rid of them. It'll keep me from having to move...which isn't gonna happen anyway!"

Doing his utmost to inform and light a fire under the pelican, Beach Cat pulled his mired paws from the sand, settled parallel to Peter, and dealt him a heaping dose of 'endeavor' by laying his spiritual cards on the table. "Listen-up," he directed; "I've got restrictions on my powers and I can't do anything about those twisters! Therefore, unless the Wisdom contacts me and allows me the use of my weapons, we'll have to be self-sufficient. So please, don't give up, Peter...ya gotta make some kind of an effort...it's what the Wisdom likes to see! From what he's told me in the past, he's the most discerning employer in the universe and he's only looking to recruit individuals who try to help themselves and others, and also those who strive to hold their own against earthly adversity. Out of respect for his wishes and rules, you'd best cast-off your docking lines and get moving...c'mon...follow me!"

Ignoring the command, Peter stayed-put and doted on the conflict he had with his leader's lecture. "SQUAWF ~ SQUAWF...Enough - Enough!" he cackled. "I don't care whether the Wisdom wants to hire me or not, Beach Cat...I'm not looking for a job! If I was, and had to prove my worth to him, I'd make it clear that I already held my own and did my part by rescuing that kid...and if the fact that I'm too tired to help myself doesn't make the grade, then I don't know what else to tell ya, except to leave me alone and get out of here...before its too late! Yeah, don't get bogged down by me...save yourself!"

For an instant, Beach Cat dwelled on the derisive pelican's poignant gesture. Categorically, it registered as quality gallantry. Still, it wasn't what he wanted to hear. Forced to take more drastic measures, he cut to the chase and tried to ready his companion for an unpleasant flight of sorts. "Peter, I'm not about to turn ya over to the wolves!" he decreed. "Forgive me for hurting you, cuzz you're coming with me no matter how bad it's gonna feel. Just keep in mind that I'm not mad at ya and this is nothing personal!"

Acting on his premeditated contemplations and least damaging calculations, Beach Cat opened his mouth, lowered his head, and 'SWUMP,' he clamped his pointed teeth onto the wincing pelican's back, off-center of highly delicate areas. Utilizing his vice-like jaws and strength of a tiger, the hefty Maine Coon buttressed himself with his brawny legs and easily raised Peter's heavy body off the ground. Following a little jiggle to secure the shaken limp bird in his mouth, he put his limbs in motion and dashed northward!

Meanwhile, as the charging feline and his bulky long-billed passenger faced the dual tornados, 'C-R-R-RACK ~ KA-BOOM ~ KA-BAM,' their thriving lightning was sailing here, there, and everywhere. Since leaving the water, their winds had prospered as well, reaching close to one hundred miles an hour and continuing to rise!

Hence, along with the hardship of having his vision partially obstructed by blowing sand, driven rain, and Peter's floppy-winged torso, Beach Cat had to guard against being sucked into the vortexes or roasted by their thunderbolts. In a ploy to put some distance between himself and those extremes, he swerved to the east and headed for the populated far-side of the beach.

Once he ran out of open terrain, he scaled a steep grassy embankment and began to painstakingly negotiate a strip of breezy neighborhood backyards. Though they were cautiously void of live activity, they remained cluttered with a gauntlet of inanimate obstacles. With his line of view hindered, the tomcat fought to get around a multitude of wooden and wire fences, dense bushes, and cold ash-swirling fire pits. Intermittently, during his chaotic journey, his maneuvering skills would also be tested by a road-blocking array of picnic tables, patches of sharp sand spurs, and a handful of wide-based palm and citrus trees; one of which happened to be the orange tree that allied him to his unworldly powers. The familiar landmark prodded him to cope with his hurdles and press-on with his Herculean task. Due to his undying perseverance, he soon saw a light at the end of the tunnel, swung back onto the beach, and successfully lugged Peter over to their home sweet home!

Presently standing in front of the cave's four-foot high by three-foot-wide entrance, a reception committee consisting of Dune, Fred, Charlie and an arm-extending Larry courteously moved aside to show the door to their incoming companions. First to accompany and speak to the passing Maine Coon and his impaled pelican appendage was Dune Dog. "Whoop ~ Dee-doop ~ Dee-doo...Beach Cat!" he bellowed. "Talk about a hot-rod with paws and time-trials at Daytona, that was some kind of running you were doing! You really know how to burn rubber, don't ya?! For what seemed like an eternity, we lost sight of ya and thought ya might've taken cover in someone's garage, but I guess ya didn't need to make any pit stops. And just so you're uh...you're aware of it, me and the other guys would've liked to have given you a hand, but we're too slow to keep up with you. Not to mention, we all would've been done in by those twisters! Luckily for Peter, you were able to fish him off the beach. If he had to rely on us, he'd have been taking a fast trip to Tornadoville!"

Apportioning more compliments and comments, Dune engaged the ruffled-looking sea bird, who'd just been set on the cave's dry grounds and released from the grip of Beach Cat's incisors. "Ahoy there, Mr. Tugboat!" he beckoned. "It was pretty commendable of you to help that kid on the float! I'm sure he appreciated the tow job. As I was just telling Larry before you made your acrobatic return, your tactics probably kept him from getting swept out to sea! By the way, you old buzzard, you did save him, didn't ya? He didn't drift away from ya, did he? If he did, then you'll have to report it to Larry...and he'll chop you off at the knees for dropping the ball!"

"Dune, hush your mouth!" retorted an indignant Peter. "There's no reason for Larry to get upset with me. If anything, I'll get his applause for holding onto that kid's float and hauling him directly into shore...and believe you, me...it was no walk in the park! Yeah, with my body and wings getting blasted by hail, rain and gusts of wind...and that chubby dead-weight boy never lifting a finger to paddle his raft, for all I had to do, it nearly wasted me!"

"Well, thank goodness your troubles weren't in vain!" exclaimed Dune. "Given what you did for him, Peter, I'd say you deserve a medal...which puts you right up there with Beach Cat, cuzz for everything he did, he should get one too! And if the glory-pie's gonna get cut and served evenly, I think Larry and yours truly should get a medal for our good deeds today!"

Exploiting the canine's words, theoretically, an advancing Larry carried the torch much further. "To reduce your roster of who should get a medal, Dune, I already have one...the best there is! If any of you are interested in earning a real keepsake like mine, then maybe you should try qualifying for the Olympics. I don't know about Fred and Charlie, they don't seem to be of the correct mold or have the fiber for it. With the abundance of talent and guts the rest of you have though, you'd probably make team U.S.A! Under my management, ya might even bring home the gold…the silver or bronze would be nothin' to laugh at either!"

Distinguishing his ideals from Larry and Dune's, in tandem with catching his breath, Beach Cat modestly downplayed their hullabaloo. "I'll tell ya what, you guys…it's always gratifying to know my work is appreciated, but serious or not, all of your competitive locker-room talk of medals and glory-pie is out of my league! It doesn't…doesn't do anything for me…it's not my cup of tea. Contending with talent, guts and what we accomplished, in my eyes, I think almost anyone would be…would be capable of doing an extraordinary award-winning act or…or would even have a shot at qualifying for the Olympics if they were motivated by a treacherous storm! Yeah, there's something about waterspouts and tornados that gets the blood flowing and body cranking. Need I say more?! Now, if you'll be kind enough to excuse me, I'm gonna towel-off, tidy-up and make myself presentable…I got pasted again and I can't stand this unkempt drowned rat look!"

Progressing on to his all-important personal grooming, the Maine Coon pranced to the rear of the cave and dispelled an influx of water from his matted fur. Following that, he sat himself down and raised a paw to brush his whiskers and rid his agitated mouth of an odd number of minute feathers. Just as he was about to get to licking and cleaning his soiled legs, his grimacing pelican roommate came calling on him. "Yoe, Beach Cat," uttered Peter; "I can't tell ya how much I owe ya for comin' to get me! I'm uh…I'm sorry I put ya on the spot and gave ya fits out there…however, you have to take into consideration that I'm just not up to snuff and no where near my normal pleasant self. Anyhow, despite the grief my spastic wing muscles and the holes ya put in my back are giving me, I'm still glad to be alive and kicking! Thereby, once again, thanks for the cab ride…it was worth the fare!"

"You're more than welcome!" responded a smiling Beach Cat. "Ya know, in retrospect, Peter, I'm convinced that along with the euphoric feeling I'm experiencing, your taxi ride was meant to be! Simply put, 'Mr. Tugboat,' because you took it upon yourself to help someone else, it all came back to you in turn. To get more in-depth, it reinforces the Wisdom's teachings of reaping whatever you sow! Obviously, if practiced righteously, it's a way of life that can be quite rewarding and self-satisfying. It leads me to say if I had to do things over again for you, I wouldn't hesitate. Only next time, I'll bring along a serving of Charlie's hot sauce and guacamole to spice-up your feathers and body. Don't take this the wrong way, but it was all kind of bland-tasting…much different than any other bird I've ever had!"

Interrupting and contributing yet another verbal flavor to the mish-mash, up and coming Charlie and Fred plated their jovial thoughts. "It's good you and Peter are still in one piece, Beach Cat!" said Fred. "It's also good to have everyone inside the cave. In this fortress of ours, we can loaf-off, chew the fat, and not have to worry about what's cookin' outside!"

"Fred really hit the nail on the head," concurred Charlie. "We're definitely sitting pretty! Even with those nasty twisters tearing-up the beach, they should never be able to touch us. All we have to do is wait 'em out…they oughtta be on their way in just a matter of minutes. I'm guessin' they'll move back into the ocean and dissipate. Under the circumstances, any meteorologist would confirm my prediction as the standard rule of thumb."

Spreading their confidence where needed, the two spunky sea critters sauntered over to their cuddling and fearfully quiet female houseguests, who hadn't budged an iota from the cave's side wall. After giving glassy-eyed little Emma and her pale-faced mother a couple of reassuring winks, they headed for the center of the cave. Once there, they crawled over a rise of rounded rocks and waded into their sunken brackish-water pond. It was then when Fred happened to come up with an idea; an idea which was humorously relevant to the lingering danger outside. For even greater interest, the flippant thought he was about to unsheathe would make for somewhat of an unpopular motion. "Hey, Charlie," he whispered, "let's uh…let's tell some jokes. I've already got one in the pipe…its about tornados!"

"Sounds peachy to me," capitulated the crab. "I've been working on one about tornados myself...let's get-it-on and see whose is best!"

Dreading Fred and Charlie's gag-telling history repeating itself, an eavesdropping Dune Dog, who was standing near the pond, rudely stymied their provocative plans. "RUFF ~ RUFF...Stop - Stop!" he barked. "We've already been there and done what you guys are conspiring to do, so spare me from your drudgery! By this point," voiced the retriever, "you should know your jokes are off-limits on this planet of ours for the rest of your lives, whether I'm around to enforce it or not. Furthermore, if you were listening to what Beach Cat just said about reaping what ya sow, which you've heard before, then it'd behoove ya to shut your mouths! Talk about loose lips that sink ships, you know all too well that whenever you blow your dimwitted horns, there's usually enormous consequences to pay... isn't there, Fred...isn't there, Charlie?! Of course there is! Should we uh...should we discuss it for the umpteenth time? You're darn tootin' we will...and I don't want either one of you mouthing-off until I'm through blowin' my own horn! Don't mind me for beating a dead horse," expressed Dune, "but when you told your alligator jokes a couple of years ago, didn't it cause a gator to come out of a storm drain and attack people on this beach? It sure did! Did a beach-goer end up getting a broken and mangled arm from that gator? Yes, he did! And to put that European tourist out of his misery and keep him from having to go to the hospital, who's the one who came along and healed his arm? It was Beach Cat, wasn't it? It sure was! And after that, when Beach Cat, Larry, and myself formed a posse to chase down that alligator, of all places, where did we find it? It was on Jake the landscaper's back porch...where it had Jake and his free-loading pet mouse cornered...didn't it?! Yes, it did...and if Beach Cat hadn't intervened by putting the whammy on that ornery reptile with his power-bolts, it probably would've made mince meat out of them... which considering their dislike for us, might have been in our best interest...but still, I wouldn't wish something like that on anyone! Okay...I'm finished going over the gator episode," said the sated dog; "let's move on to some other jokes ya told. We'll uh...we'll skip the one's about fleas and fire ants...they make my skin crawl...and I'd rather forget about the infestation ya brought upon this beach! But, when it comes to those jokes ya told about sharks last summer, did they or did they not cause a shark attack in the water near Larry's lifeguard station? Of course they did! Did someone have a big hunk bitten out of their surfboard over it? Yes, he did! Was that surfer and other people in the water fortunate enough to overcome your voodooism and get to shore before they were eaten by the shark? Yes, they were…just by a hair! And in the end, while that shark was still looking for victims, who's the one who blew it to smithereens before it had a chance to put the hurt on someone? It was Beach Cat…again, he had to bail you out for those jokes too! Man oh man, Charlie…man oh man, Fred…if everything I just listed was ever publicized, there'd be a lynch mob outside our door…and we all know who they'd be looking for, don't we? And that's only the tip of the iceberg, which takes me back to how ya got me going on this stuff in the first place…and that would be the weather around here. I'm still hot under the collar and ready to lynch ya over what happened shortly after ya told your shark jokes…and I'm not about to let you guys slide on it, or give me your alibi that global warming and the ocean air currents were behind it! Yeah…if I remember correctly," rambled Dune, "your climate-related captions were about a tropical storm and bad-boy hurricane that were supposed to bypass us. Well, they didn't! Instead, right after you said your jokes and mocked those storms, they made inexplicable u-turns and then plowed into Sunset Beach. At our expense, your idiotic antics got us flooded out of our cave twice in the same month. It mortifies me to admit it, but it was almost enough to drive me to drink again! Now…in light of all the earlier damage ya caused and what's already been dumped on some of us today, the last thing we need is for you dunder-heads to put the jinx on us by saying something that'll bring down the house! Am I being crystal clear…or do I have to keep haggling ya…or maybe get Beach Cat to back me up by giving his annual input on the matter…is that what it's gonna take?! Well, let's have it, you guys…I'm allowin' ya to talk…so uh…so give it to me straight…I'm all ears!"

Feigning their innocence, the longwinded canine's mendacious joke-addicted turtle and crab friends put on the gloves and duked it out with him. "I'll give it to ya straight, Dune!" said Fred. "Charlie and

I have never put the jinx on anything…and it's getting monotonous for me to have to repeat this over and over…it's slanderous for you to pin those attacks or the movement of those storms or…or any of those other anomalies on us! Your way of thinking leaves much to be desired, pal…and I can't tell ya how much of a chore its been to have to live with you ever since you've decided to blame us for whatever goes awry on this beach. What's next, Dune…are ya gonna hold us responsible for all the world's misfortunes? I'm certain you will! I'm as certain as certain can be about this too…your rotten abusive impudence still won't prevent me and Charlie from having an occasional good time!" argued the turtle. "We always have and always will conciliate with you about our music, but you'll never stop us from telling jokes…which is what we're about to do!"

"Yeah, Dune," said Charlie, "you can talk about how we're doing wrong until you're ninety-years-old and takin' on the look of a wrinkly Sharpei…but whether we have your approval or not, we're gonna keep up with our off-the-cuff quips…it's what we've always done…it's what makes us who we are! Besides, if ya have any common sense, it should tell ya that everything that cropped-up in the past was all just a coincidence and would never happen again…at least not in this century!"

An obstinate and testy Dune brusquely reaffirmed the crab's prediction. "G-R-R-R…I know it'll never happen again in this century, Charlie…especially with me prohibiting your bad-luck jokes…and I do prohibit 'em! If you and Fred can't accept that, then just try defying my order and see what it gets ya! C'mon…give-it-a-go…keep putting your gall where your mouths are…I dare ya!"

In an arbitrary move to resolve the embroiled trio's heated stand-off, Beach Cat ceased licking his fur, took a short stroll, and with his outstretched paw, he playfully swatted at Dune Dog's nose. Upon drawing the pensive retriever's attention, he exercised his opinion in a consoling manner. "Easy now, Dune…I don't mean to hassle ya, but I think ya need to loosen your noose on the goose and control yourself! Granted, from all ya talked about and some of the other strange events which have taken place around here, your hard feelings are understandable…that's because its been bugging me, too! And you know as well as I do that it even bugs the Wisdom. Obviously, the 'corrective discipline' he said to give it hasn't worked. Henceforth, I say, instead of beating a dead horse, what we should do is just let nature take its course and hope that one of these days, Fred and Charlie will get the message and rectify their ways. However, as far as the here and now goes and what they're up to, I won't condone it, but I'm not super paranoid over it. In contrast to us getting walloped by those slow-moving storms last year, this storm should stay within the lines of Charlie's quick-hit projection...and 'knock on wood,' I don't anticipate a flood or any kind of carnage stemming from him and Fred telling jokes about it. And as they were saying, with everyone inside the cave, we should be golden! All the same," he continued, "for good measure, while those two doof-balls are doing their thing, I'd be willing to stand guard outside the door and keep an eye on the beach, just so we can stay abreast of what's going on out there. In all reality though, there's absolutely nothing for us to be afraid of...if we have a problem and can't get a handle on it, then the Wisdom's spirit will notify the Wisdom, who promised me earlier he'd be around to lighten the overload...and that's as 'golden' as it gets for us!"

Influenced by the orange-eyed tomcat's optimistic lobby, lifeguard Larry fostered the political atmosphere by casting a ballot for comedy within the ranks. "If I may cut-in, dudes," he uttered, "I'd rather not step on Dune's toes or condone what's getting his goat either, but if we've got the Wisdom to catch us if we fall, then hands down, I could really go for a few laughs right now! Yeah, even though the mountain of reservations I've got about Fred and Charlie's track record are counseling me not to do it, I'm willing to give them another stab at disproving their reputation."

Harboring sentiments that were ripe with downright disregard, an ailing, irritable and outspoken Peter chose to hop on the campaign's momentum-gathering bandwagon. "I could care less whether someone loosens the noose on the goose or who gets their toes stepped on!" grumbled the foot-stomping pelican. "I'm siding with Beach Cat and seconding Larry's motion. Let's scrap the social anxiety and have a hardy Mardi-Gras in here...before I go ballistic and bite someone's head off!"

Electing to go against the majority's flow, Dune remained opposed to the turtle and crab's risky sideshow. To solidify his stance, he exonerated himself from any repercussions. "I don't wanna be held the least bit responsible for this fiasco!" he proclaimed. "And I sure don't wanna acquire an ulcer or be decapitated from fighting about it. So, you guys can go ahead and do whatever ya want…just don't ever pretend I didn't warn ya about the possibility of something bizarre happening! There…I said what I had to say. I cleaned my closet and made my last stand…I've got nothing to add."

With their debate over the controversial subject coming to an acerbic close, excluding Beach Cat, who was exiting the cave, everyone held their ground and let Fred, Charlie and nature take their course. Promptly, Fred inaugurated the festivities by prepping his peers and bringing his joke to bear. "Okay…ready…set…get into my mojo…cuzz here we go!" touted the turtle. "Stumbling and bumbling their way through an area filled with peaks and valleys were a pair of dumb tornados who were in desperate need of glasses," he began. "Because he was nearsighted and oblivious to anything more than three-feet ahead of him, one of the tornados was forever bumping into things and getting injured! Although his much smaller but assertive-growing companion had lousy vision himself, he was fed-up with following the lead of his dictatorial buddy and running into this, that, and everything else as well. On that particular day, the larger of the two tornados was about to have another accident." 'Watch out!' cried his trailing partner. 'Stop…you're gonna get hurt!'

"Unfortunately," uttered Fred, "the poor-sighted twister ignored the warning and 'KA-POW,' he smashed into a big hill!"

"After seeing his friend taking his lumps," resumed the turtle, "the other dumb tornado was sure not to make the same mistake. Therefore, in order to avoid injuring himself, he reduced his speed, carefully skirted around the hill, FELL OFF A CLIFF, and 'KA-POW,' he crashed into a bunch of trees, shredding his funneled body!"

The sudden slam-bang ending to the Loggerhead's tale drew an animated reaction from his claw-splashing pal in the pond. "CLARNK ~ CLARNK ~ CLARNK!" chuckled Charlie. "Fred… you just…CLARNK ~ CLARNK…you just told a real humdinger!"

he bellowed. "You're jokes are...are top-shelf! They...they always crack-me-up! CLARNK ~ CLARNK...I never get tired of them! CLARNK ~ CLARNK ~ CLARNK...I can't stop laughing!"

"SNARK ~ SNARK ~ SNARK!" snickered Fred. "I'm glad ya liked my story, Charlie!" said the tickled turtle. "It only...SNARK ~ SNARK...only took me a couple of minutes to put it together. It was...it was almost impossible for me to keep it inside...I...I couldn't wait to get it out. I knew you'd get off on it!"

Funny as it may seem, in response to the shenanigans of the laughing, gasping, and drooling sea critters, little Emma and her mother sat passively while the other deadpan companions defined their disenchantment. "I don't want ya to misconstrue this as sour grapes, Fred," voiced Dune, "but in my book, I'd classify your joke as a dud. Those couple of minutes it took for you to put it together wasn't worth the minute it took for you to tell it!"

"I've heard better myself," disclosed Larry. "You guys are gonna have to pick it up a notch...otherwise, the hook's comin' out and the curtain's goin' down!"

"Yeah, rack-up another one and make it good!" demanded Peter. "Get a move on...tell me a joke that'll make me laugh and take my mind off of my injuries! Or for that matter, to kill two birds with one stone, I'd like to hear something that'll make me forget about my hungry growling stomach! Am I asking for too much or what?!"

Hoping to placate the apathetic crowd and make amends for Fred's inadequacy, an under-the-gun Charlie commandeered center stage. Once he'd collected his quirky thoughts, he briefly scanned his on-lookers, wiped a splotch of regurgitated clam remains from his mouth, and opened his can of worms. "Alright, you guys...here's what I've got for ya!" commenced the crab. "It was Saturday night and two tornado brothers named Dribble and Bibble were going out on separate dates with twin sisters! Having to travel a long distance through all sorts of farmland, the brothers chose to take their own short-cuts and meet-up on a main thoroughfare. Thus, while ignorant Dribble glided over an onion field, an older and more intelligent Bibble flew across an inviting area that was planted with sweet corn.

"After reuniting with each other," said Charlie, "Dribble complained about the short-cut he'd taken." 'Man...those onions I went over gave me a terrible body odor!' he groaned. 'I could use some deodorant!'

'PEE-YU…you're not kidding!' assented a good-smelling Bibble. 'You'd better make room for me and keep down wind…I can't stand the stench of onions!'

"As the tornados hustled through more farmland," continued the crab, "many an acre into their journey, they came upon their anxious dates, who were both up for grabs. At the time, one of the good-looking tornados was waiting above an apple orchard. Nearby, her clone-like sister was hovering atop a patch of garlic. Suddenly having an uneasy feeling over what he was seeing, Dribble, who still reeked of onions, made a remark to smitten Bibble." 'I suppose you're gonna stick me with the garlic chic,' he uttered. 'I can tell by the way you're creeping toward that apple girl!'

'Well, I just love the scent of apples!' replied Bibble. 'By itself, it should answer your question as to who's gettin' the garlic chic! But just think, Dribble, because of your onion aroma, you and her should be a perfect match for one another. Best of all, you'll never have to fret about any other guys coming onto your honey-pie…and vice-versa…your honey-pie won't have to fret about any other girls coming onto you!'

'Yeah…right,' muttered an irked Dribble. 'Thanks for your contribution, big brother…ya just brightened my day!'

"Later, after returning home," said Charlie; "stinky Dribble was quite happy and had no qualms about his night-out with the garlic girl. To his bewilderment, however, he noticed Bibble looked depressed and was mumbling something about his mirror-image date." 'So, what's with you?' inquired Dribble. 'Didn't ya care for the sister ya picked? I thought ya loved the scent of apples!'

'Apples my butt!' retorted Bibble. 'Like we did earlier, before she got to where I first laid eyes on her, my deceptive date took a short cut of her own and happened to saturate herself with a real strong odor!'

'What'd she do…go over the cherry or the plum orchard I saw at the other end of that farmland?' asked Dribble. 'Boy, if she did, then she must have really smelled dee-licious!'

'No, you airhead!' howled Bibble. 'She flew over a 'pasture' and it made her smell like COW POOP!'

Following the joke's punch-line, loud laughter and favorable reviews echoed throughout the cave. "SNARK ~ SNARK ~ SNARK!" snickered Fred. "Charlie, that was great!" he bellowed. "It was even better than the doozey you told this morning about Larry and his ancient hunk of junk guitar! SNARK ~ SNARK ~ SNARK...you really know how to tell 'em, don't ya?!"

"HARNK ~ HARNK ~ HARNK!" giggled Peter. "Yeah, Charlie, ya gave us a winner...it's what I'd...HARNK ~ HARNK...it's what I'd call a keeper! Hey, its a pity we don't have a camera," mentioned the pelican; "look who's laughing now!"

Peter was gawking at and channeling Charlie's eyes toward an amused and defused Dune Dog, who'd openly succumbed to the crab's performance. "HARF ~ HARF ~ HARF!" chuckled the retriever. "Ya know, if we're able to survive this amateur comedy routine," he uttered, "I'll mosey on up the coast to Madeira Beach and tell Charlie's joke to a friend of mine...he'll savor it! Coupled with that, you can bet I'm never-never-never ever gonna date a cattle dog...or one of them squalid sheep-tending Border Collies!"

To an extent, lifeguard Larry and the young mother that he rescued were also laughing over and enjoying the crab's joke. On the whole, their emotions were heightened by a rip-roaring and endearing little Emma. Remarkably, she appeared to have recovered from her wretched romp in the water and "TEE ~ HEE ~ HEE," she was giggling and wiggling in her mother's lap like only a five-year-old could giggle and wiggle! Hail to dunder-heads, despite any previous derogatory jeers, Fred and Charlie's humor seemed to fit the bill in regard to easing the tension created by the storm.

Countermanding to the engaged gathering temporarily losing identity with the thorn-in-their-side weather, they were about to be given a stirring refresher by an alert Beach Cat, who'd detected something peculiar evolving between the frisky enduring tornados and relayed his discovery through the cave's ajar doorway. "Hey, tone it down in there for a second, folks!" he hollered. "I hate to interrupt your joke-fest, but if you can break away from what you're doing, then ya oughtta take this in...you can catch it through the palm trees!

I can't say if it's more of Fred and Charlie's voodooism…if it is, then I doubt it's anything for us to be excessively alarmed about. For all it's worth, if ya get up here and dabble in this, ya just might find it exciting…but I'll leave that to the eye of the beholder!"

Acting on the Maine Coon's alluring come-hither, everyone turned serious, deserted their tranquil pond setting, and headed for outside.

Upon emerging from the cave, Larry, Peter, and Dune were utterly shocked to see what was transpiring on the beach beyond the wind-damaged lifeguard station. "Whoa Nellie!" exclaimed Larry. "I think we're about to experience a rare occurrence!"

"Rare or not," voiced Peter, "it's giving me the heebee-jeebees! I'll tell ya another thing, it's nice to be here and not down there!"

Stricken by déjà vu, Dune Dog, whose tail had drooped between his legs, harmoniously commented on the latest happenings. "Wow… talk about head-on collisions! I'll have to agree with you, Peter…it definitely gives ya the heebee-jeebees…which is exactly what I was feeling not too long ago, when I was on Treasure Island!"

Next to materialize and stand amidst the spellbound group was little Emma's circumspect mother, who was still holding her daughter. Once the woman had raised a hand to shield Emma's face from the rankling rain-riddled wind, she looked off into the distance, where she saw a chilling jaw-dropping sight. "Dear God," she gasped; "that's unbelievable!"

Last to consort with the crowd, poky Fred and Charlie showed-up in time to witness the two south-bound funnel clouds fully merging with one another. The unexpected union resulted in the formation of a virulent 200 ft. wide vortex! Its sobering appearance drew a daunted response from the watchful turtle and his crustacean chum. "Holy moley!" cried Fred. "Are ya seein' what I'm seeing, Charlie?"

"I'm logging it," confirmed the crab. "It's pretty funky! It's kind of spooky too…I hope that thing stays far from us!"

Doing just the opposite, 'CR-R-RACK ~ KA-BOOM ~ F-R-R-ROOM,' the newborn lightning-flinging storm skipped into the ocean, took on a northeasterly gait, and lumbered for the cave!

Conspicuously, on the fringes of its blustery path, Larry's tiki hut was rocking, reeling, and shedding what was left of its bamboo, palm frond and plywood skin. Because of its vulnerable location and malleable construction, it was destined to suffer total annihilation. In brutal fashion, tersely, the wee structure was wrested from its stilted foundation and whisked into oblivion!

Further down the beach, a custom-made flag that was tethered to an aluminum pole was ripped from its moorings and sucked away! The now defunct piece of colorful cloth, which displayed a large orange bursting with juice and jagged lightning, had been specifically designed, commercially ordered and strung-up by an artistic Larry. Called the Flag of Justice, it symbolized Beach Cat's rapport with the honorable Wisdom. Although it managed to survive the lesser winds of the twofold tornados, like Larry's work station, it fell prey to their beefy offshoot.

As he eyeballed the cyclone and evaluated its ferocity, Dune Dog saw the earmarks of a potential calamity and nearly jumped out of his fur! Right away, he took control of the situation and herded everyone inside the cave, where he stood at the head of the class and vigorously vented his pompous lesson. "G-R-R-RUTT...Dog-gone-it!" he growled. "I told ya so...I told ya something bizarre would go down," reiterated the retriever. "Only this time, because of Fred and Charlie's bad-luck jokes, we could be in dire straights! Man oh man, from watching the Stormy Planet Channel at Larry's bungalow, I can guarantee ya that if that compressed hurricane keeps its course, we're all gonna wish we were somewhere else...and so will all those who are living in this area!"

Perplexed by the dismal update, Beach Cat stepped forward and gullibly expressed his ignorance to the speaker of the house. "What in tarnation are you talking about, Dune? You've got me at a loss for logic. Why would we want to be somewhere other than in our cave? I thought Fred and Charlie said we were good to go in here! And didn't you say we had the best shelter around for this type of storm?"

Being astute to the tumultuous outside conditions, Larry intervened and elaborated on the dog's forewarning. "What Dune's implying, Beach Cat, is the fact that this twenty-foot cave isn't deep enough to prevent a funnel that size from getting at us. From what I surmised, its girth is almost half the width of this beach! If it comes back ashore, the same thing that happened to my hut and your flag, could easily happen to us! I uh…I've already thought about making a run for one of the homes or condo units around here…it might be a redeeming avenue for us to take…if the funnel doesn't tag along. If it does, then odds are, our new sanctuary would be demolished. So, it's my contention that we should stay where we're at…there really isn't any other site in town that's more solid than this! However, no matter where we are or what we do, there's still a possibility we all could be…could be uh…we uh…"

Taming his lax tongue, Larry found his interest drawn toward little Emma's mother and her skin-clinging daughter. Masked with looks of horror, they were gazing back at the lifeguard, listening to his rambling with great diligence. Concerning overall moral and the manic vibes radiating from the gals, Larry chose to scuttle the latter part of his death-related hypothesis. "Well, I guess we're uh…we're just gonna have to start thinking positive and be confident with our environment," he concluded. "Its got my endorsement!"

Meanwhile, after conferring with Fred about Dune's haunting objections to their stories and the serious wake-up call they were getting, Charlie candidly confessed his remorse over the dilemma everyone was facing. "Look, you guys…it's…it's tough for me to admit this, but I guess the jig is up, and I'm awful sorry for what I did and for what's goin' on! I assume this won't mean much to anyone, but if I could erase the joke I told and make everything better, I would…in a jiffy!"

"What goes for Charlie goes for me," sustained Fred; "and we ain't just whistlin' Dixie! We're truly sorry for sinking the ship with our lips…it seems we've got a knack for doing that."

Ticked-off, snorting, and keying on Fred and Charlie's earlier arrogance, Dune Dog, who was hip to Emma and her mother's mood and wanted to safeguard them from his pending rhetoric, ushered the reactive cowering turtle and crab aside. Confidentially, he proceeded to give them an earful. "Guess what?" he whispered. "Our ship hasn't sunk just yet! Be that as it may, I could maul myself for allowing you to have your way! You guys don't know when to quit, do ya? You're always determined to be a blight on society and make yourselves the center of revulsion, aren't ya?! To shorten a long story, you're disgusting…you're the scourge of the south…and if it wasn't for all the new crime-solving techniques and the forensic evidence I'd leave on you space cadets, I'd do the Mexican Hat Dance on ya's and turn ya into tortillas! It would put a stop to you and your jokes, which aren't so funny now, are they? I should think not…but that's all inconsequential! Because ya wouldn't listen to me, real soon, we just might be lifted off our feet and yanked out of this…"

Before Dune could finish flaunting his discipline, 'FA-WHOOSH,' he and his holed-up companions took a big body-bending hit courtesy of the storm's outer winds. As the squinty-eyed group stood stunned in their tracks, suddenly, all around them, they saw the cave's lightweight contents become airborne. Presently being skimmed and blown out of a pair of stainless steel feeder bowls were dried bits of ricocheting cat and dog food! Simultaneously, two small matching blankets, which belonged to Beach Cat and Dune Dog as well had been converted into flapping flying carpets and were sailing overhead. Down below, in addition to everyone getting drenched by a steady spray of infiltrating rain water, 'WHISSSS,' abrasive sand pelted, stung, and then clung to their wet bodies!

Challenging the paralyzing effects of the gale-force winds and irritating elements, an on-the-move Larry aimed to alleviate the pressing problem. "Hold on, everybody," he shouted; "I'm gonna try to patch the leak!"

Pushing with everything he had, "OOMPH," the gasping lifeguard was barely able to close the cave's moisture-warped slatted door, which he secured by lowering its spring-loaded two-by-four deadbolt. By design, Larry had built the fully-framed triple-hinged barrier from heavy oak and was now glad he made it nice and sturdy. For the time being, his strenuous effort eliminated all but a wisp of the wicked wind. Nevertheless, with panic burgeoning in the dank dimly-lit cave, both an affected Fred and Charlie, who were unaware of their leader's dearth, inadvertently hit the same sore spot by assailing his inactivity. "Hey, Beach Cat," beckoned Fred; "how come you're not out there taking-on the funnel with your power-bolts? And why didn't you use 'em earlier when Peter was in trouble? What's the deal with you anyway…are ya gonna strike-up your claws and get me and Charlie off the hook for this mess or what?"

"Yeah, Beach Cat, whatta ya hesitating for?" queried Charlie. "It's a no-brainer that ya need to unleash your lightning and cream that thing! If you get rid of it for us, I…I swear to you, Fred and I will never tell another joke…plus, when this is over, we'll take a swim and catch you some scrumptious Grouper…your favorite!"

Ironic to what the shamefaced turtle and crab had previously stated, Beach Cat parlayed his sincere apologies with a germane evaluation. "I'm sorry, guys, but I can't offer any help. To put ya in the know, I'm unarmed and I can't do anything except wait for the Wisdom to give me permission to use my weapons, if they're necessary! Not to worry though…as I mentioned before, if we get into a bind, we'll be taken care of…we can bank on it. The rest of this town can bank on it too! On that basis, let's uh…let's all try to relax and make like we've got some faith."

"Well, Beach Cat, I can't find any room in my head for relaxing or having faith!" countered a revitalized and fully cognizant Peter. "Jumpin' jittery toads on a busy road…I just survived a close encounter and I'm not thrilled about having another one. All I can say is that the Wisdom's spirit or even the Wisdom better not snub us…otherwise, the whole lot of us will be gutted and churned into milkshakes…without the milk!"

Dune Dog exemplified his fine feathered friend's prognosis. "Peter ain't lyin' about the milkshakes…talk about threats to homeland security, all of our lives are in jeopardy! Nothing against you, Beach Cat, but if I was the one who slurped-up that premium orange juice and was in your position, I'd tell the Wisdom to quit fooling around and get with it…I'd order him to give me my weapons pronto…and I'm sure Peter, Fred, Charlie and Larry would do the same!"

Prior to airing his thoughts on a not to be neglected issue, in deference to Beach Cat's angelhood, Larry quashed the contagious dissension; wherein he castigated Dune's final inclusive remark. "Alright, men…shut your traps!" he commanded. "Your barnyard henpecking is for chickens and losers…and I won't tolerate it! Let me tell ya something…if any of us trigger-happy ya-hoos had the use of those power-bolt weapons, then we probably would've obliterated half of Florida by now! Most likely, it's the reason why the Wisdom takes to Beach Cat, who seems to be the most even-tempered and self-assured out of all of us. That should go without a single argument! At any rate, no matter what the Wisdom or the future brings about for us, I suggest we stop jawing at one another and get organized. If we're gonna be under fire, then we'd better take advantage of what we have to work with and get ourselves to the rear of the cave. How's that for an intelligent proposal? Does anyone here wanna question me or gripe about it?"

Indubitably, as they all pulled up stakes and moved their door-side camp, the majority of the group was fraught with gruesome thoughts and were scared to death. To the contrary, an intrepid Beach Cat's lone bothersome tribulation was his well-shared but personally concealed impatience. Forget about him acting cool and collected on the outside, in his muddled mind, he was desperately seeking punctual support from the results of his prayer in the water. "Wisdom...where's your help?" he asked. "I did what I could for you today and I don't deserve to be put off! So, what's the glitch...what's your spirit tellin' ya? Where's the storm gonna go? Why don't ya talk to me...are ya even around?"

Sensing no reply to his intolerance on the sly, he lowered his head in disappointment and continued to follow his migrating companions.

Soon thereafter, with everyone spotting themselves along the cave's back wall, 'WU-R-R-R-R-RUMBLE,' they heard a demoralizing train-like sound growing loud on the beach. It was the shore-breaching funnel telegraphing its imminent arrival! Consequently, its earthshaking approach sent terror-induced tears streaming down little Emma's puffy cheeks, which were gently wiped-away by the cold trembling fingers of her sure-talking mother. "It'll be okay, sweetie," she uttered. "I've got you in my arms and nothing's gonna happen to you!"

Also taken down a few notches by the menacing storm, Peter wound-up his webbed feet and 'THUMPITY ~ THUMP ~ THUMP ~ THUMP,' he waddled close to Fred and Charlie, where the pessimistic pelican let it all hang out. "Listen to me, ya mischief-makers...just in case the Wisdom leaves us high and dry, I'm takin' this opportunity to say I'm really gonna miss the two of you! I'm gonna miss doing our girl-watching and clam digs together. I'm gonna miss our daily and disgraceful lid-flipping garbage can raids on this beach. I'll even miss the fights we have with Jake the landscaper over us roosting here…which shouldn't be for much longer. I guess if things keep going the way they are, then once the funnel slams into this cave, it should be finished with us pretty quick…which would be for the best, I suppose."

From a defensive foxhole he and Charlie were struggling to craft in the cave's hardened floor, Fred flung scrapings of loosened sand with his flippers and then took a recess from his digging to share similar thoughts with the pelican. "We'll really miss you too, Peter! Like you're figuring, once the funnel hits, it'll be all she wrote. That's the good part…the bad part is what's gonna take place in advance. Yeah, just thinking about having my tonsils extracted through my nose is extremely unnerving. It's actually making me nauseous…to the point where I could easily blow my cookies. Suffice to say, I'd rather not have anyone talk to me face to face…it'd be wiser to just send me a fax!"

Resting his soiled claws to get to the brass tacks, Charlie dejectedly abandoned his tedious excavation project and expressed his anguish over the seemingly hopeless situation. "This is it for us, fellahs…there's no tomorrows. Ya know, we've all been around for a while and had a great life. It's just too bad it's gonna be nipped in the bud…cuzz I'm really wantin' it to go on! I wanna live…I wanna live forever…with you guys!"

In conjunction to Charlie's mournful declaration and to the rest of what he heard, on behalf of everyone in the cave, Larry thumbed the mark of a cross on his forehead and quietly prayed to God. Afterward, he advised his comrades to huddle-up, hit the deck, and do whatever they had to in order to survive. Conversely, in an act of selflessness, the lifeguard stooped low and draped his body over Emma and her mother, affording them maximum shelter from the powerhouse storm!

Knowing the crucial moment of impact was drawing near, Dune Dog minded Larry's recommendation by walking, stopping, and dropping within inches of Beach Cat, who out of frustration had distanced himself from the others. Itching to reveal his innermost melancholy feelings, reluctantly, Dune crooked his sand-covered head and face toward his aloof counterpart. In the darkness of the cave, he focused on the prone Maine Coon's luminous eyes. "It's uh...it's time for me to submit my good-byes to you," resigned the retriever. "I wish this wasn't happening to us...I wish I wasn't about to cry...and if I don't get this out in a hurry, you just might see my levee rupture. So, here goes...in a nutshell, if we don't make it through this, then its been a real pleasure to have made your acquaintance! We uh...we go back a long ways, and I can vividly recall the day I came to your rescue and pulled you from the water...you were in La La Land and couldn't talk...you weren't movin' much either! When Larry took ya over to his girlfriend at the animal hospital, I never thought you'd make it. Somehow, ya did, and I'm happy we had our stint with one another. For me, it was great from the get-go...and I could think of a better ending for us. I'm sure you could too! To tell ya the truth, when I talk of a better ending for us, that duh...that revives an old conversation I had with some people about reincarnation, which is something I've been bandying about ever since. If there is such a second dimension to this world, then maybe we'll meet again sometime in another place. That would be boss, wouldn't it...us meeting in another place?!"

Though Dune's valediction was well-appreciated, it was unacceptable to an unresponsive Beach Cat, who wasn't about to give up the ghost or look past the present. Rightfully so, for as he lay in defiant limbo and listened to the hellacious funnel cloud, all at once, he heard a domineering and unmistakable baritone voice that was audible only to an angel. It was the Wisdom. **"Heed my words!" shouted God. "My spirit has informed me of the rouge tempest becoming all too predictable. No thanks to Fred and Charlie, its route will tally more senseless destruction and evoke death...clearly, it must be stopped and held liable! Oh mighty cat, prepare to raise your paws and intercede with your claws. In the name of justice and for the protection of the meek, do what you must...use your warranted skill and defile that aggressive essence of evil...reduce it to dust...permission has been granted!"**

Upon receiving the Wisdom's blessings, 'BA-ZOOM,' Beach Cat's front claws turned warm to the touch and started to grow and grow and grow! With untold speed, they tripled in length, filling and brimming with supercharged lightning. Combined with his strength and courage of a tiger, in a flash, the stoked-up feline was fully ready for battle!

Firmly adhering to his pledge, in clockwork fashion, God's assistance arrived just in the nick of reason and a few nervous heartbeats. When all was said and done, 'C-R-R-RACK ~ FA-WHAM,' both a wood-splitting and lock-busting one hundred and sixty mile-an-hour torrent of air blew the cave's door wide-open. Almost immediately, the compromised cave depressurized, its fractured misaligned door was belted back toward its frame and 'C-R-R-REAK ~ KA-BAM ~ VOOM,' everyone inside was enveloped by the roaring storm's vicious circumnavigating vacuum! The blockbuster intrusion was more than sufficient to push little Emma over the brink. From beneath Larry, she appealed to her primary overseer. "Mommy...Mommy! Don't let it get me...please... don't let it get me!"

Besides having the 'big squeeze' put on her, Emma was given strict orders. "Hold on to me, baby!" stressed her mother. "Don't let go of me no matter what! Do ya hear me? Don't let go!"

In its own right, now closing-in and tightening its grasp on the cave, the heavy-breathing water laden funnel began taking a life-threatening toll on its vulnerable victims. Having his existing instability intensified by excruciating pin-pricking pain, Peter the pelican, who was crouched alongside a dug-in Fred and Charlie was first to falter. "SQUAWF ~ SQUAWF...Help...Help!" he cackled. "It's sucking my feathers off...I'm getting plucked alive!"

Comparable to Peter, Fred was being dragged over the coals by the unforgiving wind. "Someone had better do something!" voiced the desperate turtle. "It's sucking me from my shell...it's ripping my head off!"

Adjacent to Fred, Charlie writhed and moaned in agony. "OOOH ~ AAAAH...it's pulling my...my legs out of their sockets!" yelled the crab. "I'm getting torn apart at the seams!"

Enunciating cohesiveness, stubborn Larry, who was scratching at the ground and straining to maintain his coverage over the curled-up mother and daughter, urged everyone to stay with the program.

"Don't give in to the storm! Fight it off together…f-f-fight it with everything you've got!"

Derailing Larry's pugnacious pep-talk, 'WOOSH,' an accelerated surge of thieving manhandling air-pressure rushed inside the cave, putting Dune Dog's receptive ears on maximum alert. To the cringing, paw-skidding and dejected animal, it meant only one thing. "That funnel's coming for us!" he cried. "We're all gonna die!"

Aroused, hurting, plotting, and begging to differ with the dog, Beach Cat sprang-up on all fours and asserted his superseding belief. "You're wrong, Dune…we're not about to die…now batten your hatches and hang-in-there while I'm gone!"

Throwing caution to the wayside, 'SH-R-R-ROOM,' he sped toward the front of the cave with a vengeance!

Initially, no one was aware of his liaison with the Wisdom. As a result, an on-looking blurry-eyed Dune was flabbergasted by his cohort's actions. "What the…have ya gone daffy?" he shouted. "Whatta ya gonna do?"

Just before he was sucked from of the cave, Beach Cat glanced back and gave Dune a much longed-for response. "Got my p-p-power-bolts…Wiz-z-z-z-z-z-dom!"

On that drawn-out and waning note, 'VOOOSH,' he disappeared through the cave's entrance, which after undergoing a thorough skinning and cleaning by the storm was totally void of its door.

Door or no door, as soon as Fred and Charlie had processed their vanishing on-a-mission leader's utterances, they started to go bonkers! Despite his subdued and lack of breath condition, Fred managed to muster some encouragement from his deflating lungs. "B-B-Bring it on, Beach Cat!" gasped the turtle. "K-K-Kick that twister's butt!"

Plagued by breathing problems as well, sassy Charlie joined Fred's rally by standing and pointing ahead with his rip claw. "Hey, B-e-e-e-each Cat," he wheezed; "tell the…tell the twister it smells like cow poop!"

Due to the wrenching wind and his reckless punch-line send off, the Stone Crab found it quite difficult to get down into his shallow makeshift bunker. Ultimately, in attempting to do so, he lost control of his wavering exoskeleton frame, fell to his left, and inadvertently plunged one of his spiked feet into his turtle friend's face. "Yee-ouch!" yipped Fred. "Charlie, you c-c-clumsy oaf!" he screeched. "Quit thinkin' about your c-c-cow poop joke and get off of me...or you'll get the heave-ho!"

Literally leaning toward keeping the status quo, Charlie placed his safety before the Loggerhead's wishes. "Fred, I don't wanna move my leg...if I do, I'll lose my footing and get sucked-up by the t-t-twister...it'll twirl me into cotton candy! Please...g-g-give me a break...I can barely hold on as it is...and if ya got any sympathy in ya, you won't blow your gooey cookies on me...if ya do, it'll make me slip!"

Suffering from both a hyper-extended neck and a sharp claw buried in his sunburned eyelid, Fred spouted-off with yet another pain-driven wisecrack. "Ya know s-s-something, Charlie? If the storm does anything, I hope it sucks off all of your...your skinny legs...especially the one that's spearin' me!"

"Right b-b-back to you, Fred!" countered the crab. "I hope your... your mouth gets sucked-off so I don't have to listen to it! But it doesn't matter...I can't do this forever...before long, I'll be...I'll be off of your p-p-pickle-puss...then, you'll get what ya asked for!"

Indomitably, with salty Fred and Charlie and the remainder of the languishing grotto-bound group being sapped of their strength, outside, the monster twister was growing stronger! Currently carving a broad swathe in the beach, it was inhaling sand by the truckload, methodically stripping the soft granular ground all the way to its hard-shelled core. Adding to its land-based feast, slowly, it descended upon the dense nestle of bowing palm trees that were fronting the cave. Violently, one after another, 'R-R-R-RIP,' it began to uproot and swallow them whole! At the same time, from its belly, successively, 'B-Z-Z-Z-T ~ B-Z-Z-Z-T,' the storm released an explosive pair of sizzling lightning bolts. Perilously, they coursed for negatively-charged pay dirt.

A split-second later, near the cave's entrance, 'KA-WHAM,' a deep fissure was burrowed in the ground by the leading bolt of electricity, sending smoldering melded sand, a glut of pebbles, and a plume of sparks high into the air! Bringing up the rear, 'VR-R-R-ROOSH,' the second yellow-colored thunderbolt snaked its way indoors and

'KA-BOOM,' it slammed against the cave's back wall, narrowly missing a low-lying Dune Dog and company. The lightning's resounding ear-piercing noise was rivaled by two blood-curdling screams, which came from the quivering mouths of little Emma and her mother. Likewise, out of sheer fright, Dune was yelping, Peter was cackling, and an unintelligible Fred and Charlie were babbling incessantly!

Saddled by unbridled anxiety himself, from his location atop the mother and daughter, lifeguard Larry, who'd been flogged and cut by orbiting pieces of pulverized rock, had already begun his second recital of the Lord's Prayer.

Save for a short nail-biting delay, soon enough, Larry's persistent plea to heaven would be answered by way of an unseen Beach Cat, whose bold external exploits had placed him in the tempestuous bowels of the windy and rainy mega-voltage melee. At the moment, the beleaguered but confident feline was affixed to the leeward side of a tall palm tree, one that was on the tornado's hit list! To his good fortune, after he'd been unceremoniously siphoned from the cave, he was able to halt his forward momentum by extending his claws and latching onto the tree's upper trunk. However, with gloom and doom looming, it was imperative for him to make his move and take the bull by the horns.

Thus, having the prior burden of retreat lifted from his thoughts, an offensive-minded Beach Cat launched himself sideways, spread his limbs Flying Squirrel style, caught a downdraft, and from close to thirty-feet up, 'WHOOMPH,' he was blown earthward, plummeting and tumbling head over heels! Crashing hard, 'THUMP'…"OOF"… he landed paws first in a tree-free zone and rolled behind a large and somewhat protective fossil-laced boulder. From well below the four-ton object's crescent-shaped apex and what just so happened to be his preferred nightly perch, Beach Cat gathered his senses and stood on his hind legs, mimicking the stature of a riled Grizzly Bear!

The Maine Coon was now shedding fur by the handful as the storm's conforming winds whipped around the boulder and tore at his bushy-tailed rear quarters. Fending-off the F-3 assault, intensely, he tapped into his jungle-cat strength, held his rickety balance, and jacked his front paws overhead. Once he'd steadied and locked them onto his expansive mile-rising target, 'FL-L-L-LICK,' he brandished his elongated claws! He then lowered his ears, bared his teeth, and "HISSSS ~ GR-R-ROWL," he let-out with a double-fisted snarl. In disdain to the funnel cloud's unwelcome advances, his pre-fight actions were leading to an angry hasta lavista! Spontaneously, 'BOOF,' the tips of his claws ignited and glistened like sparklers on the Fourth of July. Indeed, with much at stake, Beach Cat's firework show was about to begin, for in the twinkling of an eye, 'FA-ZOOM,' streaks of white-hot lightning raced from all ten of his pointed appendages!

Packing an interstellar and supreme heavenly punch, mercilessly, 'BAM ~ BAM ~ BA-BA ~ BAM,' his barrage strafed the twister both high and low with immeasurable amps of gripping electricity. Quickly, the dark whirling dynamo entwined itself with the radiant spiritual plasma and was wrapped tighter than a fly in a spider's web! Though it continued to spin in place, astonishingly, it was stripped of its wind and was no longer secreting its hostile lightning. Meaning, it was hopelessly beset by God's wrath; an ire that was being administered by the most powerful animal on earth!

Barring the noisy rain, silence and calm had temporarily fallen upon the area as Beach Cat waited for his proficient corporal juices to recharge his depleted internal arsenal. Whilst the color of his eyes flickered from orange to green to orange again, he converged his elevated paws and got set for round two. Holding nothing back from his counterattack, he opened the floodgates on his claws and 'FA-ROOM,' he cut-loose with a ferocious fusion of lightning. No doubt about it, the 'last rites' were written all over it!

Pouring on the heat, 'Z-Z-Z-ZAP ~ SPLAM,' his searing weapons penetrated and diffused throughout the hovering vortex, voraciously spreading into its vast upper crown of clouds. Instantaneously, an enhanced and near-blinding glow encircled the feline's foul-weather foe! Starting at the very depths of its hollow core and neutralized eye-wall, the once formidable behemoth was burning-up and would soon self-destruct, for only God and his elite army of angels were capable of holding that much energy.

Going out in a shrinking blaze of misery, one second...two seconds...three seconds and 'FA-BOOOM,' the towering twister imploded into an innocuous mist of steam and pure-white dust! In the wake of the blast, 'WHOOSH ~ BR-R-RUMBLE,' a massive shockwave blew an exposed Beach Cat flat on his back, bounced off every building around and shook the shoreline for miles on end!

With its swift demise and long tie to the sky severed, gracefully, the tornado's tepid remnants drifted down and began to settle upon the shifted sands and mellowing waters of Sunset Beach. Wouldn't ya know it…after the Wisdom delivered the goods, rectitude had been duly served and the turbulent threat was perpetually vanquished!

Relieved that peace had once again presented itself, Beach Cat recouped the breath that was knocked out of him, rose from the gritty ground, licked his raw nose, and briefly assessed the telling aftermath of his supernatural handiwork. Basing his closing motion on the spoils of his victory and safe seal of approval, he referred to the unambiguous rules of his heavenly trade by calling on the Wisdom to rescind his angelic powers and restore his earthly sense of normalcy. As he shimmied, kicked, and attempted to free himself of debris, miraculously, 'FOOM,' his claws, body, and eyes regressed to their usual size and color. Following his conversion, he heard an inspired cheer coming from Peter, Fred, Charlie and Dune, who'd witnessed his thunderous grand finale and were whooping-it-up from the cave's threshold.

Furthering their exultation, under clearing skies, the wind-ravaged group trickled onto the beach to convene with their leader and expound on their deliverance. Foremost to do so was a front-running and head-shaking Dune Dog, who was flipping his inversely-blown stiffened ears back into their proper loose-hanging positions. "RARF ~ RARF ~ RARF…Thanks - Thanks - Thanks!" barked the indebted canine. "Man oh man…talk about stress and premature aging, Beach Cat," he uttered; "let's hope Fred and Charlie do away with their jokes and we never have another day to match this one…I don't think I could take it…these rickety bones of mine would never be able to meet the criteria! Hey, I just…I just got another flashback…do ya recall me talking about us 'meeting' in a different place? Well, I gotta say, I never reckoned it'd be right here…which is quite acceptable to me…it's much better than pushing up sea oats and keeping company in the beach cemetery!"

Trailing the retriever and verily adding to his comments, an extremely hungry and born-again Peter, whose chafed bare head and shoddy body was minus feathers galore, had a new mind-set about life. "Hear me out, Beach Cat!" he implored. "Besides having regrets for what I said earlier, I have to tell ya that forever more, I'll always believe in you and the Wisdom...I should've never doubted you guys...ya make an excellent team! I'm glad ya went to bat for us...and to get myself involved as a player in your lineup, I'm gonna do whatever it takes to improve my job résumé...if ya get my gist! Yeah, it might not have done me any good, but when I was lying on the beach, I could have at least used my legs to get up and run from those twisters. It's something I won't mention if the Wisdom ever schedules me for an interview! Anyhow, with the storm kaput, I'm really looking forward to doing some fishing and marathon eating...that is, after I give my tender muscles and thinned-out wings a thorough testing to see whether I'm able to fly or not! If I can't, then I'll have to resort to my garbage picking habit. It's either that or I'm gonna have to pester Larry to splurge on a batch of frozen seafood dinners for me. One thing's for sure, Larry will have to keep me supplied with sunscreen until the feathers on my head grow back...it'll keep my naked noggin' from getting burned! Oh, and while I'm on the subject," voiced Peter, "I don't wanna hear any baldy jokes...mainly from you-know-who!"

Speaking of the irrepressible devils themselves, handicapped Fred and Charlie were next to approach the Maine Coon. Struggling to walk with his partially disjointed legs, Charlie was limping, wincing, bumping into Fred, and semi-clowning all at the same time. "Jeepers creepers...our neighborhood's gettin' to be awfully noisy and dangerous these days!" announced the crab. "I can stomach just about anything, but I'm not too keen on having lightning bolts flying through our living room. You could say it's a good excuse for selling our cave before it loses its value. On the brighter and more equitable side of our infamous evening in paradise, you really unloaded on that blow-hard dirt duster, Beach Cat, didn't ya?! When ya blew it up with your power-bolts, the concussion bowled us over and gave me a headache...without exaggerating, that big bang had to have been felt clean-up into the Panhandle! To say the least, ya did a dynamite job…and as long as ya didn't cause expensive structural damage to this town and there weren't any passenger or weather planes in those clouds ya took-out, you should keep your good standing and get your accustomed praise in the beach's Sun and Journal newspaper. Now, I'm uh…CLARNK ~ CLARNK…I'm not trying to start another conflict or insult ya, my friend," said a giggling Charlie, "but I can't get over how funny it was watching you, Larry, and Dune swimming into shore and running around out here today. Yeah…CLARNK ~ CLARNK…I can't get it off my mind…it was pretty hilarious!"

Dwelling on a past event that centered on his marred pickle-puss, an incensed Fred stopped dead in his tracks, glared at the immersed crab, and sought to turn the tables on him by ripping and ribbing him about his leggy miscue in the cave. "Charlie, you ditzy dork…be quiet!" he snapped. "Because of you stepping on me, my eye is almost swelled shut. If ya noticed at all…I can hardly see out of it…it's extremely painful too! That's okay though…eventually it'll go away and I'll forget about it. Then again, there's one specific incident I'm never gonna forget or let you live-down! What I'm talking about is the scared expression on your face and the way you were freaking-out when you were worried about the storm sucking you up and twirling you into cotton candy…it was just as hilarious as anything that happened today…maybe even more-so!

Charlie wasn't about to let his livid partner in comedy get the best of him. "Oh yeah, Fred, in keeping with the topic of sucking and facial expressions, you should've seen your distorted mug when the tornado was jerking and stretching your head into the next county… and there's more to your elastic trip to another zip code than what ya might think! In just a few hours, you'll be suffering from whiplash. If you were smart, before your neck muscles stiffen-up and your head falls off, you'd crawl over to the nearest health club and get yourself a long soothing massage! If ya need any supplemental therapy, then I suppose I could always whack ya with one of my claws and give ya something that'll get the kinks…"

During the turtle and crab's bickering, wild-looking Larry appeared within the congregation. After escorting Emma and her mother from the cave and leaving them to their own devices, he was looking to join the tricks and rub elbows with Beach Cat. Bearing both a new windblown spiked hairdo and a somewhat bloodied and sand-blasted body, Larry was grinning from ear to ear as he saluted the Maine Coon with great zeal. "Yoe, ya little fireball...you did it... ya booted-up your lap-top lightning and saved all of our hides! For your battlefield bravado, we'll never be able to thank you enough... and I for one, will always be respectful of what you've got going for yourself! However, with all due payback, I'm gonna get my licks in by laying the same sort of critique on you that ya laid on me about not wanting to be a full-time ocean-going lifeguard. I know your goal is to please the Wisdom and I'm not about to call ya crazy for doing what he expects of you, but if I was ever given the choice, even if it was only for a day, I'd never wanna be you! Your path in life takes a lot more courage than mine and there's no way I could ever fill your shoes...or claws, to be precise...and since your weapons are on ice and can't barbecue me, you can go ahead and give me five. Here...put 'er there, my man!"

An accommodating and ever-so-humble Beach Cat reacted to Larry's open palm by slapping it with his rigid paw. "I'm flattered by your compliments, buddy," acknowledged the feline. "Still, it's wrong for you to put me on a pedestal and say you could never do what I do. If you were in my boat and were ever gifted with what's been given to me, then you'd think differently. And for all intents and purposes, it's the Wisdom who deserves a pat on the back and full acclaim for saving our hides! If it wasn't for his help, then we probably wouldn't be around to talk about the tough road we had to hoe. And you won't catch me harping about it too much...cuzz despite everything, we managed to hold the fort and avoid any severe injuries! Actually, before I jump to conclusions and let the fat lady sing...or eat...whatever way that cliché goes, I'd sure be interested in knowing how the woman and her child are doing. I just saw 'em walkin' off...their legs looked a little wobbly...are they okay?"

"Accounting for all they experienced," said Larry, "other than the same ringing in the ears that I've got, and a few nicks and dings, which are negligible compared to what's on me, they seem to be just fine and dandy! Right now, they're searching for their beach gear. From what the mother told me, together with her purse, they had a cooler and several towels lying around...plus, Emma's float took a hike somewhere. It was sucked outside along with the cave's door and I'd be absolutely amazed if it ever turns-up...ditto for your door!"

"Well, I'm not gonna lose any sleep over a missing door and float," responded Beach Cat. "It's just nice to know everyone's still functioning...and to quote what Dune said to me just a minute ago, let's hope Fred and Charlie do away with their jokes and we never have another day to match this one! Yeah, as you can see, Larry," he uttered clandestinely, "the funnel took gobs of fur off my tail-end and I can easily relate to Peter losing a lot of his feathers, only I won't be asking you for sun-block like him. What I could really use though is a swim suit to cover my hairless butt...and if ya happen to have an extra pair, man, I'll take 'em!"

On the heels of the tomcat's plea for some semblance of common decency, suddenly, a grim-faced young woman dressed in sneakers, shorts, and a tube-top could be seen running in the direction of the cave! Not surprisingly, it was lifeguard Larry's frantic fiancée, Jennifer James, who after learning of the storm on her car radio and speeding over to the beach was anxious to get the lowdown on her beau's condition.

To pause and summarily reflect on Jennifer's own state of affairs, job-wise, the thirty-four-year-old was presently one of three practicing veterinarians within the closely-knit boundaries of Sunset Beach. Well-respected by scores of beholden pet owners throughout the area, her skillful reputation and conviction to her profession preceded her. Point in fact, besides Beach Cat, many an animal would've surely succumbed to their frailty if not for Miss James doggedly nursing them back to health!

Delving into Jennifer's Florida roots, long ago, she'd left her historical hometown of Lockport, New York and its comfortable Erie Canal setting in order to study her trade in the Sunshine State's city of Miami. Eventually, after years of reading, writing, testing, hands-on training, part-time job moonlighting and leading a disciplined life, which always made time for a regular regimen of beach-going and sunbathing, she would acquire herself a hard-earned and gratifying diploma. Prior to leaving Florida and driving to northerly Lockport in pursuit of work, for a novel encounter, she decided to celebrate her illustrious achievement and newfound personal freedom by stopping off and vacationing at renowned Sunset Beach. While lying near the ocean and refreshing her tan, she happened to befriend an infatuated lifeguard Larry, who spent an entire afternoon conversing with and getting to know his compatible female water and Sol worshipper. By coincidence, when Larry's questioning enlightened him to Jennifer's field of expertise, he aptly informed her of a job opening over at the town's animal shelter, which he'd learned of through the grapevine. Unexpectedly, his hot tip instigated a flourish of activity for the petite, auburn-haired and semi-homesick Miss James. Whereupon in just a seventy-two hour period, the ecstatic vocational school graduate landed herself secure employment, rented an affordable furnished apartment, and made the cozy seaside community her new place of residence!

Since meeting Larry, for the past four years, Jennifer's devotion to animals was exceeded only by her ardent love for the lanky lifeguard. It was slow to come, but once the skeptical Olympic champion had talked himself into proposing, he and his bride-to-be meticulously tackled all the details and were slated to be married in a mere eleven months. At the moment, an emotional Jennifer had both that beckoning trip down the alter and disconcerting beach disaster weighing heavily upon her mind. Hence, after racing up to her on-looking man in waiting, she threw her arms around him, wet one of his lowered weathered shoulders with her tears, and conveyed her concern. "Honey, I was in a traffic jam when I heard about the waterspouts hitting the shoreline! I kept trying to reach you on your cell-phone and couldn't get ya to answer. My God, Larry!" gasped a recoiling Jennifer. "You're all scratched-up...there's...there's blood all over your back and neck...and some on your forehead! Are you all right?"

Besides his usual welcoming kiss on the cheek, robustly, Larry gave his girlfriend the skinny on his much-fattened self wellness. "I've never been better, Jenny!" he professed. "I'm sorry I missed your calls...as it was and still is, my phone's not on me and I hadn't even given it a thought. Yeah, things got a little distracting and dicey for a while, dear, but thanks to your favorite feline client and those trusty claws of his, like the rest of the crew here, I was able to survive. Really, I can't tell you how glad I am to be alive! And don't let my appearance bother ya too much, Jen...I might be sore on the outside, but on the inside, I'm uh...I'm feeling g-o-o-o-d! Essentially, other than my trepidation for this trashed beach, I don't have a care in the world!"

Getting more than he bargained for, the lifeguard's composed answer paved the way for an on-edge and dead serious Jennifer. "Sweetheart, I was so afraid of losing you today that I nearly went out of my mind!" she moaned. "To be frank with you, Larry, I'm awful tired of waiting...are you feeling good enough to get married tomorrow...on Sunday? I was thinking long and hard about it when I was stuck in that back-up on the road. Instead of having a huge wedding and honeymooning in Mexico, we can just elope and carry-on in my old stomping grounds! Yeah, we'll fly up to Lockport, rent a car, and have the ceremony on the overlook in Outwater Park, which is identical to what we planned...only it'll be just you, me, Joe DiBannis the red carpet guy...and Pastor Ray to marry us. Once we're finished with all the formalities, we'll buy a big bottle of champagne, take a thirty-minute ride and book a room in a waterside hotel down by Niagara Falls. The following day, after we're up and about, we'll secure a stretch limousine and cruise over to the City of Tonawanda for its Erie Canal Festival. We'll sample the boat parade and rides for a couple of hours and then we can head into the town of Lewiston for a bit of shopping and partying on Main Street. From there, we can walk to the 'Wine and Dine' restaurant along the lower Niagara River and have ourselves a late candlelight dinner. It'll be wonderful! So, whatta ya think about my agenda for us...and then some?!"

Caught off guard by his fiancée's stress-related brainstorm, wide-eyed Larry, who at one time vowed to be a life-long bachelor, nervously snapped his nylon bathing suit and rationally stammered his way through an uncontestable excuse. "Hey, t-t-take it easy, Jenny...you've lost the scent in the woods...and your uh...your idea couldn't possibly hold any water! Don't get mad at me for pulling the plug on your tub, but for what you wanna do, there'd be too many arrangements to make and not enough time to do it...which is fine with me, cuzz my system can't absorb any more tension for today! Above all, allow me to give you a little reminder...our wedding is on tap for next June and we already ordered the invitations and put a non-refundable deposit down on a banquet room! For Pete's sake, before we uh...before we lose-out on our money, skip town and...and do something that'll get our families and friends upset with us, we should put the burner on simmer and give it more consideration. Maybe uh...maybe sometime in the next couple of months we can sit down and discuss it. Yeah, we'll uh...we'll talk about it later."

Jennifer frowned upon Larry's answer. "Geeze...I hope you're not getting cold feet, mister!" she uttered. "Just remember this yourself... the night we got engaged, verbatim, you said you'd thought about it and told me it'd be a snap to leave your single days and beach bar get-togethers with your buddies behind you! You're not having a problem with your own words, are you? If you are, then maybe you should have that pre-cana conference with Pastor Ray, which you've been avoiding...it should let ya know if you're ready for a change in lifestyle. If ya happen to have any uncertainties after Pastor Ray's talk, then I'd have to question whether or not your old flirtatious girlfriend is back in town again! And now that I've brought-up 'Miss Malicious,' whatta ya have to say about her? Has she been calling you? Is she still throwing herself at your feet and tryin' to discourage you from marrying me? Does she still want ya to move to Indiana with her or what?!"

Growing agitated over having his personal business spilled in front of his intrigued and speechless cave-dwelling friends, Larry took his girl into custody, walked her in a discrete direction, and kindly read her the riot act. "Jenny, your irrational behavior might go over well on one of those TV talk shows, but it won't earn ya good ratings with me. What's more, this isn't the time or the place for giving me the third degree...it's gonna make me the main course of gossip around here! Good grief, because of what ya said, Fred and Charlie will be laughing at me and mocking me out...they'll have a field day over it!"

"That'd be sensational!" retorted Jennifer. "Yeah, maybe those two goofy groupies of yours will motivate you to get married sooner than later...like sometime uh...in the next couple of months! Better yet, when you bring Beach Cat to me for his annual physical in September, I think I'll ask him to give you a hefty rap in your midsection with his molten weapons. It may be just what you need to get rid of your butterflies!"

Larry warily balked at Jennifer's snide resourcefulness. "I'll definitely pass on Beach Cat's lightning! And don't depend on Fred and Charlie motivating me…if anything, they'll jinx me! Now, before I call-it-quits and collapse from exhaustion, Jen, let's check on what used to be my lifeguard station…and then we'll see about my home-life situation. The storm really did a number on the hut…and it'll be a wish come true for me if my cottage is still in one…"

As Larry and his significant other were strolling out of earshot from Beach Cat and company, someone else entered the area. Clad in just a faded pair of farmer jeans and a raggedy baseball hat, it was a disturbed-looking middle-aged man named Jake LaFake. The local pony-tailed beach resident had an ongoing territorial feud with the cave-dwellers and was about to have another run-in with his lazing and unsuspecting antagonists.

Originally hailing from Louisiana, stout and short five-foot-two Mr. LaFake, who previously owned a landscaping company there, had opted to relocate to far-off Florida for the sole purpose of escaping his widowed and controlling live-in mother. Mind you, from having been smacked upside the head and badgered daily by his elderly maternal matriarch for frequently neglecting his prerogatives to shave, shower, make his bed, hang-up his clothes, clean his fingernails, and cut his long hair short, Jake finally had his fill! Therefore, within an indignant span of thirty days, covertly, he sold his business for a handsome sum, carefully weighed his computer-based listings on prime resort property, swapped E-Mails with a real estate agency, packed his bags, and left his poodle-haired mother both a farewell letter and the deed to his ranch-style abode. He then hopped into his classic Cadillac and followed his print-out travel map all the way down to Sunset Beach.

At the advent of his arrival, Jake signed himself into a mom and pop motel for an extended stay, caught forty-winks, and kept an appointment he had with the on-line realty firm. Eagerly, he scrutinized their offerings, put an unbeatable bid on what was affordable and bought himself a much sought-after shoreline condominium. Whilst waiting to move into his costly spiral-staircased dream house and seeking career-oriented employment, once more, he felt he'd hit the jackpot by attaining the beach's vacant groundskeeper's job, which he had under his belt for the past ten years. Along with tending to the somewhat sparse but valuable plant life, in general, his tedious duties entailed grooming the sand, cleaning the municipal restrooms, and keeping the entire surroundings looking spiffy for persnickety tourists and town residents alike.

Other than his reputation as a perfectionist in his work ethics, the never married and characteristically low-keyed Mr. LaFake, who happened to live just a couple doors away from lifeguard Larry was also known to be slightly on the eccentric side. As peculiar and implausible as this may seem, almost any activity the salt and pepper-haired maintenance man was involved with, he'd be accompanied and sometimes assisted by his tiny gray-colored pet mouse, whose name was Moses.

Coming from a long line of preaching mice, Moses, a Florida native, had once been an impetuous wanderer, moving from place to place in search of better food, finer fellowship, and the ultimate environment to make his permanent home. Apparently meant to be, many moons ago, on a hot summer afternoon, he accidentally crossed paths with Jake on the landscaper's shady back porch. After scaring each other half to death, the two lonely souls laughed heartily, exchanged pleasantries, and soon took to one another. Before they knew it, their Saturday social hour sprouted into an affluent veranda and then house-sharing friendship. In due course, through trial, error, and thick and thin, they honed themselves to a pinnacle where they became virtually inseparable.

For example, whenever it came to beach-related chores, grocery shopping, midnight bowling and Thursday bingo playing, devout Moses could always be found riding high up in Jake's stiff-billed sports cap. Amusingly, out of natural impulse, the hyper buck-toothed critter had gnawed numerous holes in his master's head-covering, which not only helped to aerate it, but also gave it a Swiss Cheese guise. Another noticeable by-product of the man and mouse relationship involved Jake's heavy southern accent. Over time, his pronounced drawl had rubbed-off on little Moses. On occasion, particularly when the twangy-talking duo were in a tizzy, it was often difficult for others to understand what they were saying.

'Reader' beware…an on-the-march Jake was now about to put that same language barrier to the test! Upon working his way front and center of the scruffy cave-dwellers, he raised his hat to the top of his forehead, jiggled his loose upper dentures back into place, and confronted the group with his festering malice; some of which dealt with the eerie storm and its too-close-for-comfort landfall. "Hey, ya bunch of sorry-lookin' banana-heads!" he bellowed. "Ah thought y'all might've given up yer dastardly doin's, but yer at it again, aren't ya?! Somehow, ya mated those two scrawny tornaders and finagled the burly red-neck ya created into takin' a big ol' bite out of mah beach! Not to mention, it ripped the shingles off mah tool shed, blew the lid to mah hot-tub spa into the ocean, and put our playboy lifeguard's guitar through mah bedroom winder. Addin' insult to injurah, it painted mah butt with sharp sandspurs when Ah was tryin' to git mah new gas grill un-dah cov-ah! Afta Ah went inside to extract them insidious weeds with mah needle-nose pliahs, me and ma-mouse dang near got sucked out of our house! Ya know, Ah've been livin' and workin' in these hee-yah parts fer quite a spell, and although Ah've been hoodwinked by some ghastly stick-in-mah-craw weathah, Ah nevva imagined the outside elements would take a tumble the way they just did! As a mattah of fact," snarled a finger-pointing Jake, "overall, evva since you creetchas settled in this region, its been cursed like the Bah-mew-der Triangle. Land-sakes, along with this demonic Beach Cat hee-yah shootin' lightnin' bolts from his claws, there's been gator and shark attacks, tropical storms, hurree-canes, flees and fire ants in mah black-eyed peas, and now waw-tah spouts and twistas…its…its always been one theng afta anotha! Let alone the strain its been puttin' on mah mental faculties, its also been demeanin' to mah beach! Now, with me bein' a man of intellect, y'all will have to excuse me fer mah biased behavior when it comes to yer breed, but the proof is in the puddin'…and Ah've got an iron-clad notion that all the bad luck is comin' from exact-lah what Ah'm lookin' at! So, be-sods yer usual smartah-pants double-talk, just what do y'all have to…have to say fer yer-selves about what Ah just told ya?"

In reply to the angry landscaper's accusation, both a guilty and conniving Fred and Charlie, who were seeking to take some heat off of their innocent companions, did nothing but feed the inferno. "Hear me out, Jake," voiced a smirking Fred; "I've got a mouthful to say that revolves solely around you! To begin with, I can…SNARK ~ SNARK…I can see a few sandspurs still stickin' to the seat of your trousers. I gotta…SNARK ~ SNARK ~ SNARK…I gotta let ya know…it's almost as funny as seeing you fiddle with your false teeth! Second of all, to be more uh…to be more serious…and…and focus on those fleas in your peas, I think your pet, Moses is most likely responsible for them joining you for dinner. As for those other complaints of yours, they're tellin' me that you should take a chill pill and calm down! Yeah, in re-living all of our past pow-wows with you, it seems to me, you're always blubbering and going off the deep end over something that's uncontrollable."

"Fred's right, Jake!" corroborated Charlie. "You have to get it through your head that you're in the tropics and annoyances such as what you mentioned are gonna happen every now and then. Why, before Fred and I were expelled from the…I mean uh…before Fred and I left the Bahamas, there was all sorts of disruptive stuff taking place there as well. You just need to get a better grip on yourself, that's all!"

Rebuking the turtle and crab's conjecture, boisterously, Jake didn't bother to beat around the bush. "Ah'll git a bettah grip on mah-self once y'all move on!" he hollered. "Ah'll also be happy when the time comes that Ah'm not findin' clumps of animal hair, busted clam shells and chewed-up fish contaminatin' the area arown yer cave. Or, seein' yer stinkin' shoe-stickin' droppin's all ova mah beach! The latter part of what Ah just told ya goes especiallah fer Dune Dog hee-yah, who likes to clean his pipes and do his duty at the foot of the walk-bridge to mah backyard. One of these days, ya mangy mutt, Ah'm gonna take a can of peppah spray to ya and teach ya to flush yer tol-lit elsewhere! Again, Ah hate to be cynical, but it's too bad that hail-spittin' storm wasn't able to suck-up the whole clan of ya's and set ya down in anotha town. And since it didn't happen, then y'all bettah watch yer step!" warned Jake. "Thengs are gonna git rowdy arown hee-yah if we have any moe problems…and it won't be the weathah that's huffin' and puffin' and blowin' its top…it'll be me! In plain English, it means when y'all least expect it, Ah'll be comin' into yer cave to put a good whoopin' on ya's! If it ain't enough to scare ya away, then Ah just mott have to raise the ante by sendin' fer mah eighty-year-old nag of a muthah and havin' her pay y'all a visit. She ain't all that big and ya wouldn't thenk it, but she can be a real body-bruisin' rough-how-zah. Just to give ya a little clue, she hits even har-dah than Ah do!"

Displaying a similar but more stable attitude toward the cave-dwellers, "EEK ~ EEK," a squeaking on-the-scene Moses clambered out of a front-side hole in Jake's hat and tossed his opinion into the ring. "Mah dear fellow animals!" summoned the mouse. "This beach is spacious enough fer all of us and ah surely don't wish y'all any harm. How-evah, just to keep Jake from poppin' his cork and to make life less hectic, Ah've been prayin' evera-day fer y'all to hit the road and take yer black cloud with ya! When ya do, the first theng Jake and I are gonna do is turn this place into a reputable resort. We'll be lookin' to seal-off yer dirtah cave and run a bull-doza over yer moebid cemetery…where y'all have been buryin' yer deceased friends. Afta we abolish and sanitize what ya left behind, the next theng we intend on doin' is throwin' a pig-roastin' hula-dancin' beach bash in rejoice of yer exodus!"

All the belligerent down-talking bought a resentful rebuttal from an attentive Dune Dog, who in getting his dander up was far more blatant and much less cordial than Fred and Charlie. "Moses, you and your greasy stubble-faced daddy are fraying my nerves…and ya need to stow it and withdraw to the peanut gallery…where ya belong! And just to curb your erroneous designs on us, if I was you, I wouldn't count on having any kind of a Hawaiian-style shindig to commemorate our departure, because we're not about to forfeit this land of ill-dispute. For what that entails, you'd best drop your renovation intentions and keep your mitts off of our alleged 'dirty' cave and 'morbid' cemetery!"

Still gnawing at the bit, Dune lowered his sights from the hat-bound mouse and consigned them on the rodent's human beer-bellied transportation. "As for you, Jake, ya deranged low-life slob!" he uttered. "For starters, by the looks of ya, I doubt you've got what it takes to put a good whoopin' on anything...except for maybe a brewery! Also, if your mother's a rough-houser and is able to hit harder than you, then she should have her genes examined...I'd say she's probably a 'man' and never came to terms with it! Apart from that, unless you've always been a complete ignoramus, it should be obvious to you that I only do my duty near your yard on the days when you throw mothballs over here in front of our cave. Thus, whenever you find it in yourself to put a stop to your sordid weekly ritual, then I'll put a stop to mine in kind! Pertaining to your comment on Beach Cat," continued the canine, "what you said about him being demonic is totally absurd! For quite some time, you've been aware that he's an angel of the Wisdom of the Orange and was given special powers to protect this beach. Talk about getting real, he's the one who kept an alligator from butchering you and Moses. He also put a fast end to the shark attack we had...and if he wasn't around to eradicate that storm today, I'm sure there'd be nothing left for anyone to worry about!"

"Yeah, Beach Cat really rules around here, Jake!" chimed-in a wing-flexing Peter. "And all things considered, you and your hot-shot pet had better heed Fred and Charlie's advice. If ya don't calm down and lose your attitudes, they might start telling jokes about ya...and ya may end up having more bad things come your way! Or even worse, something bad could happen to all of us...so, whatever ya do, don't get 'em going!"

Peter had no idea that his admonishing evaluation would strike Jake's fancy. Incredibly, his prior spiteful demeanor turned reasonably pliable. "Well, Ah'll be danged...y'all hit mah soft spot!" conceded the beaming landscaper. "It's nice to know Ah'm not the only one arown hee-yah who likes to tell jokes. Which reminds me, just the uthah day, Ah heard one of them 'knock-knock' jokes...it's a laugh and a half and ah've been dyin' to tell it to someone besods Moses! Real-lah, it's so knee-slappin' and bellah-bustin' funnah, it'll make ya pass gas...Ah can vouch for it! Ah'll uh...Ah'll vouch for somethin' else too...and don't go gittin' the wrong idea about this, cuzz Ah'll always be set in mah ways toward you creetchas...but...if Ah'm evva able to control the savage and bittah feelin's Ah've got broilin' insod of me fer y'all, at that time, if Ah'm not too bizzah, Ah'll thenk about lettin' ya's in on the joke Ah just told ya about. Rott now though, all

Ah wanna thenk about is how Ah'm gonna fix-up this beach y'all managed to mangle. Come tomorrah, Ah'll be talkin' to the Common Council about replacin' the palm trees and mounds of sand that got sucked away...but first-off, to remain in good standing with our tourists and the general public, me and ma-mouse are gonna have to walk back and git mah pick-up truck so's we can stott collectin' all the dead fish and rubble that's strewn on these hee-yah grounds."

Citing a prominent vestige of the storm which he, himself felt bore paramount importance, Moses peered over the elevated brim of his master's hat, got in his face, and made a shrewd pitch for revising their priorities. "Jake, befoe we git a burnin' obsession with fixin' everytheng fer the tourists and general public, what we really oughtta concentrate on first is the beach towel with the ducks on it that's hangin' from the peak of our house. Unless you want us to become the laughin' stock of this town, you'd bettah climb a ladder and git rid of that theng. Once its outta sight, then we can git to servicin' the grounds, which is gonna be a chore of lore and could take us fer-evva and evva...and seein' that Ah'm well into the age of a seniah citizen," specified the three-year-old rodent, "it might take longah than what Ah've got left to live...even just the strain of the job could cause the death of me!"

Concerning their messy monumental task, though Moses and Jake talked as if they were on their own, little did they know that a by-standing Beach Cat was already planning on both he, his cohorts, and without a doubt, some benevolent beach-goers to help them play pick-up-sticks. Nonetheless, with the sun currently on its way down and its useful radiance dwindling, the Maine Coon wanted to nix any kind of physical beachcombing labor. Thoughtfully, he came up with an alternative activity for all in his group to work at visually. "Hey, gang!" he voiced. "It'll be nightfall soon...and I think it'd be best to defer what has to be done around here. With how I've got it parceled-out, there's no reason why we can't get a bunch of bodies together and commence sprucing-up things at the crack of dawn, when we can all see more of what we're doing. If no one has any objections to that, then I suggest we call a truce to our disparities and seize this moment by hitting the shoreline and taking-in the sunset. Its got the markings of a good one…and before we miss it, I'm askin' ya's…why don't we do it?!"

Agreeably biting on the tomcat's sound logic and irresistible recreational bait, everyone packed-it-in, shuffled along, and assembled near the warm ocean. Amidst multiple roaming news crews and an investigative throng of people who'd returned to the beach, they genially sat and treated themselves to Mother Nature's light show. Providing an outstanding first act for those looking westward was the previously dark and violent sky, which had now turned tranquil and was colored with various shades of blue. As the minutes ticked away and the crowd's anticipation grew, rapidly, above the distant horizon, they saw the sinking sun light-up and gloriously glaze a lengthy row of cumulous clouds with a neonic reddish-orange hue! Such an awe-inspiring spectacle not only paid high homage to the beach's namesake, but also induced great raves from each of the cave-dwellers and the rest of the engrossed sightseers that were monitoring the brilliant and always unique event.

At the peak of the falling star gala, a once out-of-the-picture little Emma, who was held by the hand and led by her devoted guardian, slowly emerged from beyond and drew a bead on an occupied Beach Cat. Notwithstanding the back-tracking mother and daughter team failing to locate their possessions, during their abbreviated seaside scavenger hunt, they happened to run across and retrieve an item that stood for true nobility. Forwarding what was found and so neatly folded to its rightful owner, Emma placed a tattered 'Flag of Justice' beside the angelic leader of Sunset Beach. She then added a short speech and some literally touching actions to her presentation. "This is for you, kitty cat! My mommy told me the wind took it. My mommy wanted me to give it to you. Me and my mommy wanna say thank you for helping us!"

Graciously, in front of Beach Cat's companions, including an in-the-dark but curious Jake and Moses, the fatigued unsteady youngster eased-down onto her knees, and with her probing and grasping hands, she pulled her feline hero close to her, giving him an awkward hug. At that stage, Emma put a thick layer of possessive icing on the cake by talking straight from her committed heart. "I wish you were mine, kitty!" she uttered. "I love you lots and lots and lots!"

After hearing the familiar giggles of Fred and Charlie, who were lurking between Peter and Dune behind him, an embarrassed tongue-tied Beach Cat turned directly toward Emma in reply to her affection and special delivery. In doing so, he was met with yet another surprise. While gazing at the black girl's pretty face, he noticed that her heavy-lidded eyes were in a fixed position, staring overhead. Right away, he realized she was blind! Indeed, to her misfortune, the youngster's sight-related affliction was caused by an acute cancer-based infection. It was something her mother had vaguely alluded to earlier in the cave.

Luckily, with permission from the Wisdom, through his claws, Beach Cat possessed phenomenal healing abilities! Out of empathy, he sought an act of leniency from his spiritual hierarchy, thereby placing his thoughts on his sacred prayer. Silently, he repeated what he was taught to say. In epilog, he mutely rationalized his urgent appeal, which was redundant to whom he was addressing. "Wisdom, this little girl is in need of a cure! I feel bad because she can't see… please…allow me to do my will…allow me to shed light upon her eyes!"

Suppressing his cherub's plea, God discreetly left Beach Cat in an earthly way and via the same cerebral line of communication, he beguiled him with a prophetic vision. **"Dismiss your pity and accept that child on her own accord!" expressed the Lord. "Soon, Emma will grow to be an intelligent young woman. Eventually, she'll be her own keeper. Her destiny, least not partly yours actively, is to 'shed light' upon my solemn word by becoming one of my chosen teachers. To wit, her independence and role as a governess are mere precursors to her many tasks and set-forth measures from A to Z that will guide both herself and others to my awaiting wonders…so be it!"**

Hallelujah…Beach Cat's self-imposed lament was banished by happiness! To atone for lost time and shake the steadfast looks he was receiving for his zoned-out manifestation, the purring animal snapped to his senses, licked Emma's cheek, and fully reciprocated her kindness by whispering a restrictive message to her. "Listen, girlie…I uh…I just wanted ya to know that I love you too! And I don't care if ya mention it to Peter and Dune here…they'll be cool about it. That laughing Charlie and Fred though, well, they can get under anyone's skin and I'd rather ya not tell them what I said...okay?"

"Don't worry, kitty," she replied; "I won't tell Fred and Charlie anything...it'll be our secret!"

Following the pair's private pact, Emma found herself lifted from the sand and hoisted into the arms of her restless look-a-like mother. "C'mon, baby," she coaxed; "we gotta go...it's getting late and I want a doctor to look at you before I take you home and put you to bed. If all goes well, then we'll be back to say hello and do our part to clean this beach and...and maybe find our belongings sometime in the morning, after you've had your breakfast. Now, wave good-bye to our new friends, sweetie!"

As the smiling five-year-old flagged one of her hands and fondly bid adieu, before taking leave, her proud mother chose to share a tantalizing tidbit of information with Beach Cat and his entourage. "By the way, everyone, next month, my daughter's starting school... she'll be riding a bus and going to kindergarten...religion class too!"

Enthusiastically, the academic matter engendered a potpourri of random interpretations and philosophical addendums from an interested Jake, Moses, and the cave-dwellers. "Wow!" exclaimed Dune Dog. "School...how exciting...you'll have tons of fun, Emma!"

"Fun ain't the word!" emphasized Peter. "As adorable and nice as you are, missy, you're gonna have a bevy of 'boyfriends' in your classroom! Before ya commit yourself to any of 'em, bear this in mind...there's different types of fish in the sea...enough for you to wait for one to come by that really suits ya. When he does...snag him!"

Chipping-in pointers of their own were fruity Fred and Charlie. "Hey, Emma!" voiced Fred. "If ya wanna get a good report card, give your teacher a red-ripe shiny apple!"

"Yeah," said Charlie; "an apple would be ideal. Just make sure there's no worms in it...otherwise, ya might fail!"

Raking-in what the turtle and crab had to say, Jake LaFake smartly took their malarkey to the cleaners. In relation to Emma having success in school and for the balance of her lifelong days, through a biblical lesson and an old self-modified adage, orally, he attempted to sow a prudent seed. "Child, lend yer ears ova hee-yah!" he stressed. "Ah know yer gonna learn about this in religion class...which might give ya a bettah appraisal of it than Ah can...but don't evva disgrace yer-self by usin' an apple or any other means as an influence to git someone to do yer biddin'...land-sakes, if y'all were to bribe someone, you'd be openin' a corrupt Pandora's box. It's a box Adam and Eve wished they'd nevva tinkered with! To hitch-ya-up with the most refined way to stay ahead of the rat race those two sinnahs created, it's as simple as this...study God's book, chase yer honest ambitions, don't git too big fer yer britches, and plant yer corn er-lay. If ya stick to them guidelines, then y'all should reap a bountiful hah-vist. Without crowin' too much, me and ma-mouse are genuine proof of reapin' what Ah just told ya about!"

Preaching off his master's curriculum, from his perch atop Jake's head, Moses took Emma on a trip down his memory lane with a concise high-pitched sermon on the priceless virtue of sharing. "Hee-ya's anotha gem for y'all to jot down, sugar plum! When yer finished with yer schoolin' and begin to reap yer hah-vist, don't pennah-pinch it, give some of it to the needah...if ya do, it'll keep ya from becomin' greedah! That's somethin' mah great grand-daddah taught mah granddaddah...and mah granddaddah taught mah daddah...and mah daddah taught me!"

Lastly, an informed and suddenly uninhibited Beach Cat was tempted to disclose what he already knew about Emma's future. Instead, he resolved to put everything in a similar perspective, which he'd sincerely top-off with a personal elective. "Ya know what, girlie?" he uttered. "I have a feelin' you'll do quite well for yourself. In fact, over the years, it's my belief that your classmates and others will have much to gain from you. Even now, after being subjected to it, your innocent aura has taught 'me' to be less reserved and more free with my caring thoughts...irregardless of whose company I'm in! What I'm really driving at and wanting to get across to ya is that as far as our 'I love you' secret goes, you can forget about it! I'm glad I said it and I'm gonna make like it's totally ridiculous for me to put any restraints on such a thing. Besides, I'd say my surrounding contemporaries have the same warm feelings for you as I do!"

Sure enough, responding in a manner that Beach Cat was prepared to accept, giddy-acting Charlie nudged Fred and started on a hot-off-the-press 'feline love story' joke; or so he thought. "GR-R-RUFF... Knock it off!" barked Dune Dog. "Charlie, you reneging bagswaggler!" he bellowed. "It didn't take long for you to return to your old pattern, did it? Ya know, in lieu of standing here and picking-on Beach Cat, both you and Fred should be showing him some appreciation by rummaging the ocean for his favorite kind of fish...its Grouper...right? Who knows, if you were already out swimmin' and tryin' to bring him back a tasty meal, he just might be thinking about running his paws over you to heal your sore bodies. Whether he did or didn't do his magic, would've been left up to his and I should think, the Wisdom's discretion. At my 'own' discretion, I gotta say, all possibility of any of that is out the window! Yeah, because of your brazen insubordination, I've decided that for your punishment, I'm ordering the two of you to stay in the cave and suffer with your wounds for the rest of the night...or at least until your father gets home...that's when your really gonna get it! As a kicker to me grounding you," ranted Dune, "neither one of you are allowed to touch my boom-box for an entire week. Gee-whiz...it means I won't have to listen to your vile music for a whole seven days...what a shame that'll be! Hey...hold the phone for a minute...I uh...I just screwed-up...you'll have to excuse me for my blunder. I uh...I resist having to eat my words, but you can strike that restriction. That's cuzz I don't have a radio any more...the storm heisted it right after it sucked Beach Cat from the cave! So, I guess there ain't gonna be no music whatsoever for anyone to listen to. Oh well...I still have a bone to pick that's pertinent to your prior vow, Charlie...and I'm gonna see to it that you and Fred respect this!" hollered the retriever. "Meaning, you dudes will be toast if I catch you telling any jokes or shooting your mouths off about Beach Cat's 'funny-looking' bare butt...that goes for Peter's 'cue-ball' head as well. If word of their shortcomings gets around, it'll draw all kinds of nosy gawking people and some inconsiderate remarks, which'll make those guys feel self-conscious...so, if ya know what's good for ya, you'll stay quiet about it!"

On Dune's notation, until the next exciting adventure, the story of Beach Cat and the Wisdom of the Orange is over!